The New Jew

An Unexpected Conversion

First published by O Books, 2009
O Books is an imprint of John Hunt Publishing Ltd., The Bothy, Deershot Lodge, Park Lane, Ropley,
Hants, SO24 0BE, UK
office1@o-books.net
www.o-books.net

Distribution in:

UK and Europe
Orca Book Services
orders@orcabookservices.co.uk
Tel: 01202 665432 Fax: 01202 666219
Int. code (44)

USA and Canada
NBN
custserv@nbnbooks.com
Tel: 1 800 462 6420 Fax: 1 800 338 4550

Australia and New Zealand
Brumby Books
sales@brumbybooks.com.au
Tel: 61 3 9761 5535 Fax: 61 3 9761 7095

Far East (offices in Singapore, Thailand,
Hong Kong, Taiwan)
Pansing Distribution Pte Ltd
kemal@pansing.com
Tel: 65 6319 9939 Fax: 65 6462 5761

South Africa
Alternative Books
altbook@peterhyde.co.za
Tel: 021 555 4027 Fax: 021 447 1430

Text copyright Sally Srok Friedes 2008

Design: Stuart Davies

ISBN: 978 1 84694 189 4

A CIP catalogue record for this book is available
from the British Library.

Cover art by John Sternig
Author photograph by James Hall

Printed by Digital Book Print

O Books operates a distinctive and ethical publishing philosophy in
all areas of its business, from its global network of authors to
production and worldwide distribution.
This book is produced on FSC certified stock, within ISO14001
standards. The printer plants sufficient trees each year through
the Woodland Trust to absorb the level of emitted carbon in
its production.

The New Jew

An Unexpected Conversion

Sally Srok Friedes

BOOKS

Winchester, UK
Washington, USA

for Harrison and Olivia
my inspiration for everything

Bashert

"I don't care when you schedule my next appointment," Bernice dictated to the doctor from her hospital bed. "Except for February 11th. You'll just have to work around that date."

The doctor hesitated. "February 11th?"

"That's the day my daughter-in-law is converting to Judaism," she beamed.

Now, one month later, my mother-in-law, my source of unfaltering love, lay dead before me.

I couldn't know that in her death, all the pieces of what had brought me to Judaism would come to life. Traditions, rituals, prayer and community...in their practice I would see that my becoming Jewish was fate, *bashert* as it is known in Hebrew.

Had I not converted to Judaism, I wouldn't have been able to move through Bernice's death and my mourning with acceptance and full consciousness. The mourner's *kaddish*, the service, the outpouring from friends and family, the *shiva* — they were all instrumental in my healing. But I couldn't know that, crying into Michael's shoulder at the foot of the hospital bed. All I knew was that my beloved mother-in-law was gone.

***

I burst through the swinging door of the ICU wing hours earlier and found my husband standing in the corridor, arms limp by his side, looking stunned. I threw my arms around his neck and pulled away, studying his face.

"Where is she?"

"In the next room."

"How is she?"

"Not good."

Michael led me into the curtained cubicle where Bernice lay motionless, clear tubes suspended from her nose, her arm, the back of her hand. She looked like a marionette laid to rest. I approached her and touched her hand, which felt warm and lifeless all at once. Her balding head, with random wispy tufts of hair, reminded me all too vividly of the torment the chemotherapy had wreaked on her body.

We stayed with her, Bernice's boyfriend, and Michael's aunt, uncle and cousin joining us, the backdrop of the beeping monitors from beyond the hospital curtain ticking away the minutes of Bernice's life. I so wanted her to come out of the coma, but I had to ask myself, if she did, what would she return to? Her stage four of non-Hodgkin's lymphoma had already robbed us of her effervescence and strength. She had deteriorated rapidly, falling asleep in her chair on our last visit, a table spilling over with pill bottles by her side.

When the doctor declared Bernice's time of death and Michael leaned his head into my shoulder sobbing, when we hugged each other and walked out into the impossible sunlight, unable to fathom how people could be hurrying by and the world could continue when my mother-in-law had just taken her last breath, I wondered: What now?

Bernice wasn't just a cog in our wheel; she was the motor that made the whole machine work. The center-point person for our family, she coordinated everything from holidays to dinners out, arranging rides, making restaurant and theater reservations, purchasing gifts. At times she was the glue in my marriage.

Several years earlier I had decided to separate from Michael, wanting to walk away from the strain in our marriage caused by starting a business together and raising a newborn. It was Bernice who held us together by insisting, "First of all, when people separate they rarely get back together. And, second of all, if you separate, Michael is moving in with me — I'll whip him into shape!"

***

We had a funeral to plan. Walking into Bernice's apartment, a space that seemed eerily still without her, Michael said just one thing: "I want Rabbi Sirkman."

His voice, formidable with conviction, took me by surprise. Rabbi Sirkman was the rabbi with whom I had studied avidly for nearly two years for my conversion. While I had a close relationship with him, Bernice had met him just once, the day I became Jewish. And Michael had had very few interactions with the rabbi.

"I'll call him right away."

I studied my husband as he reached into the cabinet for the phone book. *How does Michael do this?* I wondered. Moments ago he had requested a rabbi. Now he sat on the sofa, thumbing through the white pages for the funeral home, preparing to call countless friends.

As my husband dialed numbers from his mother's worn address book, I ducked into his childhood bedroom to use the second phone.

"Rabbi, hi." I was relieved to get him on the phone immediately.

"Sally! Hello! How are you?"

"Well, actually, not so good. My mother-in-law died this morning." I bit back the tears, wanting very much to get through the conversation without crying.

"My God, that was fast. I'm sorry. How's Michael?"

"He's, well, everything. He's calling friends and family right now." I thought of my husband in the other room, re-experiencing his mother's death over and over, telling people the news, as I made this one call. "Rabbi, Michael wanted to know if you would conduct the funeral."

The rabbi was quiet for a moment. "Tomorrow is Shabbat, which means the funeral will have to be Sunday."

The rabbi visualized his calendar aloud. I knew what he was calculating, having learned in my conversion studies that, in Jewish law, the deceased is to be buried within 24 hours of death, in reverence to both the deceased and the surviving loved ones. A speedy burial ensures the loved one is laid to rest, returned to the earth, allowing the family to begin mourning. When I learned of the tradition, I couldn't imagine the stress, requiring people to travel on such short notice and forcing the family to make funeral arrangements in the span of one day. But now, from the inside of my grief, I could appreciate the wisdom of the tradition. The tasks before us seemed too much to bear — writing an obituary, selecting a casket, preparing a service, organizing a shiva, and so much more. Having the funeral underway in the next day, moving us out of the torment of planning and into the phase of mourning, seemed the most compassionate gift I could have received.

But Bernice's funeral would have to be delayed. She died on a Thursday, the day before the Sabbath. In the Jewish faith, the Sabbath, which begins sundown Friday and concludes Saturday, is considered the most important holiday; nothing is to infringe on the traditions — not even a death.

"Sunday is a tough day…Susan and I have this family thing. It's important," Rabbi Sirkman continued, thinking aloud. I could hear the struggle in his voice.

I knew the rabbi's schedule was demanding, constantly pulling him away from his wife and children. Weddings, funerals, hospital and hospice visits, in addition to his daily rabbinic duties, made it difficult to commit to family time. Weekends were rarely his to enjoy. Wednesday was his day off, hardly a day for picnics and family gatherings.

"It's okay. I understand. It's late notice." It seemed foolish, saying such a thing. When is a funeral *not* spontaneous? I felt guilty asking the rabbi for such a favor. While Michael and I were temple members, Bernice was not. The rabbi could not possibly conduct funeral services for every extended-family member for every congregant. And now I was putting him in the awkward position of having to say no.

"But," he said with audible certainty, "I want to do this for you and Michael. I'll be there. Let me figure out a time and I'll call you back."

When I returned to the living room, Michael's aunt was on the phone speaking to the funeral home. It was the same chapel that had held services for Michael's late brother, a 13-year-old child who had lost his battle with Hodgkin's disease, and for his father, who had died of a heart attack. One of the few Jewish funeral homes in Manhattan, Michael knew it was where he wanted Bernice's service.

Soon close friends began arriving, bringing bags full of food and helping us compose Bernice's obituary. Finally, exhausted and spent, Michael and I went home to Westchester and awaited his sister's arrival from California. Now we had to tell Harrison that his grandmother had died.

The late spring sky a gray shroud, our babysitter greeted us at the door as we came home.

"Hi, there!" she said cheerily. "How's your mother?"

"Um," I hesitated. "She's dead."

Her cheerfulness deflated as she expressed her shock and sympathy. I paid her and spied Harrison over her shoulder, playing with a conglomeration of blocks.

"Mommy, where were you?"

Just four years old, his intensity sometimes startled me. This moment was no different. Typically conspicuously attached to me, the architecture of his castle or city had momentarily hijacked his attention.

"Remember?" I answered. "I called you. Nana B got sick. Daddy and I were at the hospital." I motioned for Michael to join me on the rug.

"Oh, yeah." Harrison placed a rectangular block across a tall cylindrical one, daring it to fall.

"Harrison?"

"Yeah?"

"Remember when I read you that book about the seasons?"

"Which one?"

"The one about the leaves on the trees."

"Oh, yeah." Uncertain the rectangular block would hold, he slid another cylinder under it.

"Well, sweetie. Remember how leaves grow on trees, then grow full and beautiful and the whole tree lights up in green, sometimes with flowers, too?"

"Uh huh."

"And they're beautiful all summer. Then autumn comes and the leaves start to turn brown. Their stems get weak and one by one, they fall off the tree. They die. It's just how nature works."

He removed the rectangular block.

"Sweetie, look at me." I held his hands on my legs and looked straight into his eyes. "Harrison. Nana B's life is like the leaves. And today it was her time to die."

"Noooo!" Harrison wailed, folding his body over, dropping onto my legs. "Not my Nana B! Not my Nana B!"

I heard more sobbing then, and saw Michael crying uncontrollably, his shoulders shuddering. "No, Daddy! Not Nana B!"

Harrison hugged Michael, and they rocked, sitting over the toppled blocks, crying together.

***

I felt comforted the next morning to walk into the familiar setting of Rabbi Sirkman's office, where I had sat for nearly two years discussing my Jewish studies. It had always been a safe haven where the outside world dissipated, and today was no different.

"Before we start talking about your mother, I wanted to share this with you."

We sat tight in the sofa across from the rabbi, exhausted from a nearly sleepless night. Michael and I had talked into the early morning hours trying to absorb the day's events and I'd stayed up late fanatically cleaning the kitchen, not knowing what else to do with my angst until I finally collapsed and wept.

The rabbi opened a manila folder and pulled out a card. "Your mother wrote this to me last month, after Sally's conversion. It's a donation to the temple." He read from her note. "She says, 'Thank you for Sally's conversion service. It was a lovely day and I was happy to be a part of it. You'll never know how much this means to me.'"

Tears welled up in my eyes. I nodded, too overcome with emotion to speak. For the last 24 hours, and for endless foreseen days, the emphasis would be on Michael's loss. But now, just for this moment, the rabbi acknowledged the love Bernice and I shared.

"Thank you," Michael said, and clutched my hand, looking at me. "It's true, you know. It's true."

I thought about how glad I was to be Jewish, to be sitting next to my husband of the same faith. I was no longer an outsider, going along with Michael's traditions. I was a decision-maker, having an insider's view. Together we were constructing a meaningful eulogy with my mentor.

***

Seventy-two hours after Bernice passed away, we would hold her funeral. Finally, Sunday morning arrived. "You can go in here." The funeral director escorted us to a small anteroom near the chapel. "People may stop by to see you before the service."

One by one, family and friends entered the room, all hugging us, expressing their sympathies, the crowd engulfing and separating us. I noticed, in all the condolences extended, not once did I hear, "She's in a better place," something I frequently heard when Catholics talked about the deceased. It always struck me as an odd way to offer comfort during such a painful time. How could anyone find solace in the unknown, when all that is known is the vast void left by the loved one?

With no official position on life after death, Reform Judaism believes that heaven is here on earth, which is why we strive to make it a better place. It was one of the tenets of Judaism that drew me in, and I was immensely grateful for it at this moment.

It wasn't long before I became overwhelmed by the density of people, the claustrophobia intensified by the sea of somber clothing. Names escaped me as Bernice's friends embraced me. Mourners weaved through the crowd as they tried to make their way towards Michael. I became anxious, wanting the funeral to begin. After about an hour, the director cleared the room, leaving Michael's family and me standing in an empty room, stunned by the sudden silence.

The director returned. "We're ready for you. Everyone is seated."

We walked across the hall and stared at the ominous doors before us, intimidating not in stature but in what they held behind them. Propped up on an easel was a glamorous studio photo of my mother-in-law in her thirties, sitting on the edge of a settee, her hair tied in a bun and her low-cut black gown draping gracefully to the floor. It was easy to see that her years as an actress had never left her. On the table was a portrait taken for her presidency of the National Council of Jewish Women, a more recent photo that captured her radiance.

I felt Michael's tenseness and bit back tears. I glimpsed the coffin on my left and looked to my right at the crowd.

"Oh, my God," Michael murmured.

"I know," I answered, equally stunned. The chapel, a room with a 300-person capacity, was nearly filled.

As the rabbi walked to the *bema*, I noticed the lack of flowers and recalled Michael describing this Jewish tradition at his Aunt Molly's funeral.

"Why aren't there any flowers?" I had asked Michael. Why hadn't *anyone* sent arrangements?

"People never send flowers to a Jewish funeral."

"Why not?"

"Instead of sending flowers, we make contributions to a cause or organization that was meaningful to the person who died."

"What do you mean?"

"It's a way of honoring someone. Flowers are sort of a waste — they die. Contributions don't."

Looking at the closed coffin in front of me, I thought how pleased Bernice would be to have donations made in her honor to the National Council of Jewish Women, the organization where she had volunteered for the last 20 years. It struck me that, even in her death, she would continue to make an impact.

The rabbi opened with the *kaddish*, the mourner's prayer, and we all read aloud from the brown prayer books that had been distributed at the door.

Yit ga dal v' yit ka dash sh'mei rabbah.

I had heard the kaddish at Friday night services but never found it particularly enchanting. Interested in the meaning, I had sat in the pew of Larchmont Temple, reading the translation, trying to find something in its message that resonated with me, but failed.

Glorified and sanctified be God's great name throughout the world which He has created according to His will. May He establish His kingdom in your lifetime and during your days...

Now, sitting next to my husband, looking at the coffin that held my beloved mother-in-law, the message still fell flat. I wasn't much in the mood to praise God, nor express my desire for an abundance of peace from heaven. But, while the words themselves held no value, the hypnotic rhythm of the sentences drummed through me. For the first time in three days, I was without distinguishable thoughts. I wasn't thinking about the eeriness of Bernice's absence or metering how Michael was faring. Behind me sat almost 300 people, chanting the kaddish in unison for Bernice, calling out their sadness and their condolences.

Y'hei sh'mei raba m'varach l'alam u'l'almei almahyah.

I became entranced by the prayer. Infused by its serious tone, the roomful of people transformed from individuals in mourning to a cohesive community, and it was heard —we were grieving, and we were united in our sorrow.

What I witnessed next was not a lugubrious funeral but a tribute to Bernice, and a healing one at that.

"Tradition teaches," started Rabbi Sirkman, "there are those whose lives are as question marks in the Book of Life, never leaving enough of an impression to discern their impact. If this is so," he looked directly at our row, "then Bernice Friedes can be nothing other than an exclamation point...for the impression she left is indelible...it is etched upon every person here today, and countless other souls, I dare say."

The rabbi seamlessly stitched a mosaic of Bernice's life, from her childhood in Brooklyn and her relationships with friends and family to her volunteer work and broad interests. He spoke candidly, recalling my mother-in-law's difficult childhood, her strength to rise above it, and her innate ability to love absolutely everyone she received as a friend. With his anecdotes of her renting an entire theater to show Michael's student film, her balancing plastic stacking cups on her head to entertain Harrison, and others, the rabbi captured the complex essence of Bernice, evoking tears and laughter from everyone in the sanctuary.

***

The gathering at the gravesite was an intimate one, by invitation only. Because the burial is the most painful experience around the death of a loved one, in the Jewish tradition it is the most protected. Often, only the immediate family and close friends attend the burial. As the row of limousines pulled into the cemetery, I thought it strange that I hadn't been there before. For all the years Michael and I had been together, he and his mother had come to the cemetery on Yom Kippur, visiting the gravesites of Michael's brother and father. Once, when I asked Michael if I could go with them, he quietly responded, "It's something my mother and I do." Now, approaching the family plot, seeing Harry and Tony's headstones next to the third, freshly dug grave, I understood how painful it must have been for Michael and Bernice to visit here annually. I felt all too intensely the enormous loss of Michael's family.

As we stood in an arc around Bernice's coffin, lowered a foot below ground level, it made sense that this moment be reserved for those who were closest to the deceased. Her immediate family along with a few lifelong friends all shared a deep level of grief beyond words.

"Releasing those we love is perhaps the most difficult thing we will do," Rabbi Sirkman said. He reached for a shovel, upright in a mound of dirt. "The act of throwing dirt onto the coffin, letting your loved one go, is the most selfless act you will perform. In Jewish law, it is also the greatest *mitzvah*."

I looked to Michael, wondering if he was shocked to see the rabbi holding a shovel in his hand. It seemed impossible at the moment, a living horror, that we should actually bury our beloved friend, mother, sister, aunt — together. The small action of throwing dirt onto the casket was conceivable, and a mere handful seemed symbolic. But this was beyond symbolism. We would literally start to bury Bernice.

Bernice's brother, Norman, walked over to the rabbi and took the wooden handle from his hand. Digging in deep, he lifted a heap of dirt from the ground, the sound of metal scraping against the earth so basic and primitive. Taking a step forward, he tilted the dry soil toward the coffin, where it landed with a thud. We cringed collectively. Others stepped forward then and did the same. With every spadeful of dirt, I felt the pain of each individual, the brother releasing his sister, the friend letting go of her friend, the niece saying goodbye to her dear aunt. Finally, I stepped forward to take the shovel, something I absolutely did not want to do. One of the most nurturing people in my life, Bernice was a mother who cherished me, who had taken me in as her daughter. She was my role model for demonstrative maternal love, for community service, for dignity and grace. She had only been in my life for ten years and I did not want her to leave me.

I drove the steel tip into the mound of dirt and lifted it. The soil was heavier than I expected, making it difficult to leverage it with my arms. I looked down at the shiny oak box, dirt now splayed across it like colorless fireworks, and felt the strength from those who had just performed this wrenching task before me. *If they could do this, I can, too.* The presence of those around me faded away. It was just me, the earth, and Bernice. My heels sinking into the ground, I leaned forward, tilting the spade on its side, spilling the soil onto the coffin. A puff of dust burped from the soil and the smell of fresh dirt rose from the gravesite.

I was intensely grateful for the earth at that moment. Ever since childhood, I had seen God in nature, finding solace in the wilderness, on hikes, on bike rides, while camping. And now, the Jewish tradition of participating in returning a loved one to the earth made complete sense. In the scent of the soil, I felt God welcoming Bernice to the Divine folds. It was as if God were saying, "Thank you. I've got her now. She'll be okay."

Michael took the shovel next, and fell into my arms when he dropped his portion onto his mother's casket, his body shaking against mine. One by one we released Bernice, the finality emphasized as we each dropped a red rose onto her casket.

As we walked back across the grass to the limousines, arm in arm in clusters, the sun shining as if it didn't know better, one of Bernice's friends, Jerrie, touched my shoulder and said in her signature whispery voice, "Sally, my husband and I have been to a few burials before, but we've never been able to shovel the dirt onto the coffin."

I looked at her sweet, diminutive frame, all of 4 feet, 9 inches in stature, tears in her eyes. "Until today. I understood we had to let her go," she nodded, "and it felt like the right thing to do."

***

Riding the elevator to Bernice's apartment after the burial, I looked at my watch and hoped I'd have enough time to get her apartment in order before guests arrived. For the next few days we would be sitting shiva, a Jewish tradition in which the bereaved family receives guests, a sort of open house for mourners. Typically lasting a full seven days, shiva for Bernice was scheduled for three days. "That's how long we sat shiva for my father," Michael said, "I remember being ready for it to be over by then."

I hadn't been to the apartment since the day before, when we had the painful task of picking out Bernice's burial outfit. I noticed then that the apartment looked a little dusty. There were random papers that needed to be tucked away and guest towels should be laid out in the bathrooms.

Now, when I opened the door, I was struck by how the

apartment sparkled. Crystal vases of flowers decorated table tops, sofa pillows were fluffed, floors had been swept and vacuumed. Even the bathrooms glistened. When Bernice's friends had volunteered to take care of shiva, I had only hoped they would have a chance to drop off some food. Now I saw that these women, some of Bernice's dearest friends for more than 30 years, who probably hadn't cleaned their own apartments in their entire adulthood, had thought nothing of scrubbing the toilets of their deceased friend. They had descended on us like a flock of mother birds, silently fluttering, tending to our needs.

The dining room table and sideboard were covered with a lavish spread of food. Platters of bagels, salmon, fruit, sandwiches, and more, all lay out on silver platters. Gift baskets overflowing with fruit, crackers, cheeses and breads sat on the floor near the kitchen entrance, deliveries from friends yet to be opened. Hearing water running in the kitchen, I walked in to see Marion washing strawberries, arranging them on a tray. She had served more than 20 guests at Bernice's *Seder* for the last eight years, preparing a lot of the food and cleaning the kitchen afterward. I had also seen her working at many NCJW events.

It felt so good to see her, an extended nurturer of my mother-in-law.

"Marion," I said. She turned and hugged me.

"Jerrie called me right away. I wanted to be here."

Michael set the shiva candle on Bernice's writing table in the living room, a tall, glass-enclosed candle given to us by the Riverside Memorial staff. We were to light it, letting it burn until it extinguished on its own seven days later.

Watching the flame flicker, it seemed logical that one would light a candle in the loved one's absence, especially in their home. In my Jewish studies I had learned that the wick symbolizes the body, and the flame represents the soul reaching upward. The candle was to be lit as a reminder that our loved one may not always be with us physically, but her brilliance is not forgotten.

But to me, the flickering flame felt like Bernice's spirit, with us still.

***

For the next three afternoons and evenings, Michael, his family and I stayed at the apartment while people visited, paying their respects. I had little to compare the experience to, this only being my second shiva. I had visited with Aunt Joan's family when her father died a few years before. Bernice, Michael and I had driven to the suburbs, quietly entering a house, unannounced, without ringing the doorbell, a tradition upheld so that mourners are not disturbed. I immediately noticed dark cloths draped over wall hangings.

"What's that?" I asked.

"Those are mirrors," Bernice interjected. "They're covered as a reminder to leave your vanity behind."

Norman quietly greeted us at the door, wearing a torn black ribbon pinned to his lapel.

"What's the black ribbon for?" I asked Michael.

"In Jewish tradition, you're supposed to tear a piece of clothing you're wearing as a symbol of your grief. Now people wear a torn ribbon instead."

I had only met Joan's father at a few Thanksgiving dinners so had little reminiscing to do with her family. We were asked to join everyone in the living room to recite the mourner's kaddish, and within an hour we had departed. I was left wondering if our presence had offered them any solace at all.

While Bernice's shiva was less traditional — there was no daily recitation of the kaddish, the mirrors were left exposed, and the torn ribbons that we received at the funeral parlor stayed on our lapels for just one day — there were several times when I had yearned for more. When a friend approached me, repeatedly stating that I looked too thin, I finally exploded, "Well, excuse me, but I've been a bit busy taking care of my dying mother-in-law!" Had the mirrors been covered, perhaps she would have remembered that it wasn't the time to make me self-conscious about my appearance.

There is also a tradition in shiva of sitting on low, wooden boxes, reminding the survivors that mourning is an uncomfortable time. Looking over at people lounging on the plush sofa, talking sometimes jovially, they seemed to have forgotten that it was a sad time. At one point, listening to Michael's brother-in-law tell a humorous story to a group of people, I couldn't contain my tears. He noticed me crying and patted my leg.

"You must be exhausted."

I shook my head, the knot of emotion in my throat blocking my words.

"It's been a long week for you."

"It's not that," I finally managed, "I just miss her. It feels like she should be here."

Sometimes I actually felt awkward crying in front of others, choosing instead to excuse myself to Bernice's bedroom so I could weep privately.

Yet, for all my discomfort with the light environment, it was the camaraderie of shiva that sustained Michael. He was surrounded by friends from childhood, relatives from both near and far, and contemporary friends, too. At one moment, on the second day, a group of Bernice's friends were telling us stories, things we had never heard about Michael's mother before.

"...and when she didn't like someone, she'd handle them with complete diplomacy, then walk into her office, and cuss like a sailor," Bernice's secretary recalled. Michael and I exploded in laughter and disbelief. Bernice, ever dignified, had never said a bad word about anyone, was adverse to gossip, and certainly never swore — at least not around us.

"Where is Mrs Friedes?" a voice from the kitchen asked. I turned to see Marion standing in the doorway. *But she knows*

Bernice died, I thought, until I realized she was looking for me.

"I'm right here."

"I have a few questions for you about the food."

It seemed strange that Marion addressed me so formally. She had always called me *Sally,* my mother-in-law being *Mrs Friedes.* It struck me then: the role of matriarch was being passed on to me. Another wave of longing overcame me, wanting to turn back the clock so I could reclaim the security of my mother-in-law's presence. She was the one who was supposed to take care of arrangements, making decisions about all the family logistics. Did this mean that I would call Aunt Joan and Uncle Norman about Thanksgiving? Would Michael and I now host Passover? Never having to give any of these family gatherings a thought, I did not feel prepared for this role.

Walking past the shiva candle, I looked at the flickering flame and saw the spirit of Bernice winking at me. I turned, taking in the roomful of Bernice's friends and family holding plates of food, talking. I saw that they weren't just Michael's circle, they were the people who made up my life, too.

I knew then, with absolute certainty, it was bashert that I had become Jewish. Crowding the room was a community of people I had longed for, friends who showed up for each other, family who nurtured. And here, in the environment of mourning a death, the traditions of the funeral epitomized why I had chosen Judaism: it honored life. While Bernice was beautifully memorialized, the rituals around the funeral were also created to take care of all who loved and missed her, who would have to find a way to live a life without her. The tradition of a quick burial, shoveling dirt on the grave, a long shiva with food supplied for days...like holding the hand of a teetering toddler learning how to walk, the rituals gently guided us to the path of healing. In a few days we would be on our own.

It hadn't been that long ago that I had stood in this very living room, a Catholic girl from Wisconsin dating a Jewish boy from

Manhattan. When I met Michael, I had only known a handful of Jewish people in my entire lifetime. I had never imagined converting to Judaism, I had thought it impossible to join a tribe and consider it my own. Judaism seemed like an exotic culture to which I would be always an outsider, at best.

Now I walked into my mother-in-law's kitchen, through the doors she had walked through countless times, to direct her server.

"Yes, Marion?"

"Mrs Friedes, did you want me to put the roasted chicken out or save it for later?"

I surveyed the kitchen, taking in the platters of fruit, the empty glasses drying on the dish rack.

"There will be a lot more people coming after work. Let's save it for then."

I pushed back through the swinging door and took in the room overflowing with family and friends. If ten years ago, any one of these people had had told me that I would be a Jewish mother and wife, head of a Jewish household, I'd have thought it outside the realm of possibility. It had been a long, unexpected journey.

The Beginning

I had no thoughts of marrying Michael. For twelve months I had relished our cocoon of dating, spending most of our time together alone. Living in Manhattan just over a year, fresh out of the Midwest, I met my sophisticated New Yorker on a blind date. He entered the room wearing a custom-fit tuxedo, ran his hand through his dark hair and it was over. I fell madly in love.

Within days of our first date, we became fast companions, holding hands, immersing ourselves in New York City. While I had enjoyed exploring the city on my own, Michael bestowed upon me the bounties of Manhattan like a prince spilling jewels at the feet of a peasant. Together we rollerbladed through Central Park, dined in neighborhoods from Little India to the Upper West Side, and thrift shopped throughout the city. Manhattan was worlds away from my suburban home in Wisconsin and I relished every minute of my ultra-urban life with my boyfriend.

We ventured beyond the island of Manhattan, too, to the Hamptons, where Michael and I spent many summer and autumn days at the family house his father and mother had built in the Northwest Woods of East Hampton. We booked weekends at bed and breakfasts in New England, antiquing our way through small towns.

Everything about being with Michael was fun. I loved our favorite pastimes of going to flea markets, reading the Sunday *New York Times* in bed, and having brunch together at our favorite quaint restaurant. Our intimate bond felt safe and exciting all at once.

Michael courted me in a way women dream of. Dining me in candlelit restaurants, presenting me with jewelry and small trinkets for no special reason, and leaving love letters on my dresser. He called me several times a day, just to check in, and my heart jumped every time I heard his voice on the other end of the line.

I was protective of our partnership. Normally a person who loved to go dancing and party hopping, I felt no strong desire to expand our social life beyond each other. No one else's attention mattered to me. Michael listened to everything I said intently, asking thought-provoking questions, deepening our connection with every conversation. I only wanted to be alone with him. I was under his spell, happily, and he, mine. Then, after several months together, Michael asked me to dinner with three of his closest friends.

I walked into the restaurant and was greeted by three polished, stylish women sitting at a round table, waiting for us. Looking down at my jeans, torn in the knee, and my weathered black-leather jacket, I immediately felt out of place. After brief introductions, Beth, Nicky and Debbie broke into their own conversation, repeating inside jokes, reminiscing about classmates I'd never met. I knew nothing about Birch Wathen, the private school they had attended together in New York, and even less about East Coast colleges. More disconcerting, they talked freely about their salaries, rents and country houses. I was appalled to learn that Nicky and Beth spent $10,000 each to share a summer beach house with half a dozen friends. Their respective portions were nearly half my annual salary.

Spending time with Nicky, Beth and Debbie reminded me too clearly that there were differences — perhaps insurmountable — between Michael and me. He had been raised in the folds of a small, elegant, upper-middle-class Manhattan family, while I was the daughter of a Milwaukee high school teacher and homemaker.

From my teen years on, if I didn't earn my own money, I didn't have supplements to my basic wardrobe or spending money for pizza with friends.

I once asked Michael how he celebrated birthdays as a child.

"It was great," he reflected. "My dad and I would put on jackets and ties, my mom would get dressed up, and we'd go to a nice dinner followed by the Broadway show of my choice."

I had been raised in a large, middle-class family with six kids on the south side of Milwaukee. For our birthdays, we put on our shoes and went to Shakey's pizza. Our family had gone to the theater once — to hear Bill Cosby in his stand-up routine. I had five siblings, a dozen aunts and uncles, and cousins numbering over 20. Michael was essentially an only child, with two older half-sisters and a small extended family.

For all of these significant chasms in our background, there was one obstacle we never discussed: I was raised Catholic. Michael was Jewish.

We dabbled in a few more dinners and brunches with friends after that night, but ultimately, I still preferred our time alone. I liked our cocoon.

So, when Michael said, "I thought you might like to come to Passover dinner," I was taken by surprise. This was much more serious than dinner with friends. We had never discussed the need to meet each other's extended families. Michael had only met my mother and the few siblings who had visited New York in the past twelve months. The thought of spending an entire night duplicating the experience with his friends, in the closed quarters of his mother's apartment, created a sense of dread in me. On top of it, this would be my maiden voyage with a Jewish event. I hadn't even attended a Jewish wedding.

As a Catholic Midwestern girl with nearly no frame of reference for anything Jewish, I had never given Passover much thought. My understanding was that Passover was a spring celebration and that it involved a holiday dinner called a Seder.

"We'll have a few hors d'oeuvres, read from the *Haggadah* and have dinner," Michael explained. "It's a little long. But other than that, it's no big deal."

Although working-class Milwaukee seemed a universe away from the privileged Upper East Side of Manhattan, I thought it possible the Seder would resemble the Easter dinners of my childhood. The spring holiday was always an especially happy one in my household. The morning was launched with the annual hunt for Easter baskets in our four-bedroom home. Stashing baskets behind curtains, suspending them from light fixtures and tucking them into closets, my parents never seemed to exhaust their locations for concealment. After delighting in the discovery of the wicker basket marked with my name, my fingers pulled at the strands of plastic grass in search of my favorite candy — colorful, foil-wrapped chocolate eggs and cherry-flavored jelly-beans. Hand-colored eggs that we had spent hours designing and dyeing anchored our loot, but they were of little interest to us. We would hand them over to our mother to be mashed into egg salad later.

Easter was the holiday in my household that felt most abundant. My dad supported his six kids and wife on a modest high-school teacher's salary, with the occasional additional part-time job taking tickets at the State Fair or cashiering at a liquor store. My mother worked tireless hours at the sewing machine, creating wardrobes of suits, shirts, pants and dresses for her husband and kids. Christmas gifts from our parents were rationed to one apiece. Birthdays were equally conservative. But every Easter we knelt over our baskets, reveling in the found riches. The taste of sugar dissolving on my tongue was especially sweet after giving up candy for 40 days of Lent. Easter marked the reward for my sacrifice.

After breakfast my siblings and I scuttled about late morning, tidying the house and preparing appetizers for the guests of our annual holiday dinner. Moments before they arrived, we'd pick out our best dresses and shirts, ready to welcome the mix of church friends and aunts, uncles and cousins into our home. I watched in amazement as my mom magically transformed from serious taskmaster to relaxed, glowing hostess as she opened the door to the first guest. Having a house filled with laughter and high spirits was something she truly loved, and an ambience she easily achieved.

As the house slowly filled with friends and family, we kids entertained ourselves with board games and skits in the bedrooms upstairs while the adults nibbled on cheddar cheese, crackers and summer sausage below us. At 2 o'clock my mother served an afternoon dinner of ham, German potato salad, soggy green beans and store-bought sliced white bread. The moderate buffet, presented on my parent's wedding china, was displayed atop crisp, white-lace linens. Watching at least 16 people devour my mother's meal, my eyes kept tabs on the diminishing platter of ham, hoping there would be enough left to warm in a frying pan the next day for a savory lunch of leftovers.

I expected Seder to be a similar affair, sans the ham and Easter egg baskets, of course. Michael explained we would read from the Haggadah, a storybook of the Jewish exodus from Egypt, then eat dinner. But the rituals of Passover didn't really concern me. It was the thought of meeting a room full of 20 strangers that created a tightening in my chest.

The night of the Seder, Michael was to meet me after work in the lobby of his mother's building. The long, wide corridor of Bernice's high-rise complex reminded me of a museum hall. Walls of floor-to-ceiling windows flanked the expansive, rectangular room, where two black-leather benches floated side by side in the middle of the floor and square mirrored pillars stretched to the 15-foot ceiling on either side. At the door I watched taxis pick up and drop people off. Behind me, the glass walls enclosed a botanical garden with walking path, for which I could find no obvious entrance or exit. Everywhere I looked within the lobby, I saw myself reflected sitting, legs crossed, somewhat bent forward on the awkwardly low bench.

To alleviate my anxiety while I waited for Michael, I focused on the hub of activity in the lobby. Uniformed men moved in synchronization, one doorman spinning the revolving door for incoming and outgoing residents, another speaking to residents on the house phone, yet a third opening cab doors, easing fur-clad women out with a chivalrous hand. To my right and behind me the mail clerk moved about in a room filled with rows of high metal shelves. Each man acted in the gentlemanly manner one would expect from someone dressed in a starched blue-gray uniform, a navy-blue tuxedo stripe stretching down the side of the leg.

"Hello, Michael! And how are you? So good to see you!" I loved hearing the exuberance of the doormen. They seemed like a circle of uncles, lovingly descending upon my boyfriend. "I remember when you were just this tall!" They lowered their hands to thigh level. "And now here you are with your girlfriend! Always good to see you." As I watched Michael's graciousness charm the doormen, I imagined Michael's late father talking with the same group of men, possessing the same magnetism. A sudden pang of mourning overcame me, wishing I had known Harry.

Michael and I kissed, hugged, and walked through the last half of the glossy lobby to the elevator. Roger, the 30-something elevator man, held the door open with the palm of his white-gloved hand and pressed the button to Bernice's floor. I turned to Michael. I had precisely ten floors to excavate some pertinent information.

"Tell me again who will be there?"

"Let's see, there will be Uncle Norman, Aunt Joan, my cousins Karyn and Andy. Oh, and my mom's cousins Roberta, Dick, Louis, and maybe cousin Eddie. I think he's dating someone, and she may be there..."

He caught a glimpse of my uneasy smile and squeezed my hand. Our slides were moving in opposite directions on the ruler. The more relaxed Michael became as we approached his childhood home, the more my tension increased. "Don't worry. I hardly know half these people, either."

My eyes widened. If he didn't know the roomful of people I was about to meet, then how could he possibly navigate me through the crowd?

"You always manage to have a group of people around you," Michael reassured me. "You're so enthusiastic about everyone you meet." He reminded me of a recent evening at a restaurant, where both the bartender and waiter ended up relaxing with us at our table after hours.

It was true — I lived the theory that people were fascinating. I thrived on hearing where they were raised, what interests they embraced, how they met their spouses and what their dreams and goals were. My father's attitude, that strangers were simply friends he hadn't yet met, had been evident with every store clerk and fellow customer he chatted with. I had matured into an adult with the same chatty tendencies.

My method of managing introductions in any social setting was to ask questions. It was a skill that had earned me numerous top salesperson awards since the age of 16. It also kept the focus off of me. But, on this night, I would be the only newcomer to the group, which meant I would be the interviewee.

"Tenth floor," Roger announced with a nod and a subtle smile. As the door slid to the side and Roger held the open button with his cotton-clad thumb, I took a deep breath and stepped out of the elevator, finding myself all too soon in front of apartment 10C. I released my breath and slid off my overcoat as Michael rang the bell.

"Just a minute!" I heard the clicking of high heels before the door flew open and there I was, face to face with the family. There was no turning back.

"Hel-lo, darlings!" Bernice stood before us, arms lifted from her sides, an actress at the center of the stage. Her hourglass figure was flattered by black satin pants and an emerald-green silk blouse tucked neatly into her waistband. A crystal-beaded necklace accentuated her generous cleavage.

Bernice cupped Michael's face in her hands and kissed his left cheek. She looked at him as if setting eyes on her son after years of separation, but we had seen her the previous Thursday when we met for dinner on the Upper West Side. I watched with envy, wondering what it was like to feel loved like that, just for walking through the door. She released Michael's cheeks and turned to me.

"Hello, dear." She smiled with a tilt of her head. I melted as she kissed me, Chanel No. 5 curling itself around me like a genie's tail, its spell tempting me to drop my shoulders and relax.

"Was there traffic? Norman and Joan said it took them *forever* to get through the park. Terrible. Really."

"No, it was al—"

"Let me take your coat, darling." Bernice was a dichotomy. A sincere smile, a loving kiss, a question of interest, then a hairpin turn of distraction. I'd be lured by her charm, only to be released before I completed my first response.

"Juanita! Juanita. Will you please take these coats?"

Juanita walked out of the kitchen, the dark, sagging skin on her plump body a sharp contrast to her stiff bleached-white shirt, matching skirt and apron. She responded to Bernice's holler with her rubber-soled footsteps across the parquet floor and a placid expression. I suspected Juanita was accustomed to Bernice's authoritative commands. "She only cooks on Wednesdays now," Michael had informed me months earlier, trying to offset my discomfort at his having been raised with a live-in nanny, a cleaning lady, a mother's helper in the summer, and an occasional cook and laundress. I had had dinner at Bernice's before on a Wednesday evening; it had made me uncomfortable to be waited on by a taciturn courier of salads and entrees. "It could be worse,"

Michael had whispered to me, noticing me cringing at Bernice's commands to the cook. "She used to use a bell." Considering I used to baby-sit, clean houses, and serve drinks at corporate parties, it was strange to be on the receiving end of domestic service. Now I felt even more conspicuous having Juanita hang my coat just one foot from where I stood, a task I obviously could have completed on my own.

Watching Juanita meticulously drape my coat over a hanger, I was reminded of a stark difference in Michael's upbringing and mine. My family was an efficient unit. With my mother at the helm, it was run like a mix between a military battalion and a cooperative. For many families, Saturdays meant neighborhood games and sports activities. For the children in my household, Saturday free time was not to be indulged in until we consulted the chore chart posted in the downstairs hallway and completed our assigned weekly tasks. The jobs rotated each week and many a negotiation started in front of that corkboard. When I successfully traded bathroom-cleaning duty for vacuuming the floors, without throwing in any of my allowance or candy from my stash, I knew I had honed my selling skills.

Our jobs extended into our daily routines as well. In our preadolescent years we delivered our dirty laundry to the basement and later returned the folded clothing to our dressers. By junior high school we were sorting, laundering and ironing our own clothes. We took turns baking desserts, setting the table and washing the dishes.

Lazing around was a privilege that had to be earned. If my mother entered the sunroom to piles of schoolbooks and random shoes scattered across the shagpile carpet, she snapped off the television and ordered us to our tasks like a drill sergeant. "Socks. Sally. These are yours. Put them away. Books. Are these yours, Chris? Now! Upstairs!" All pairs of eyes hastily scanned the room and we leaped off chairs and scurried, with our fingertips to the floor, picking up our belongings before falling victim to the verbal lashings.

Standing in Bernice's spacious foyer, my coat taken from me by a cook-housekeeper, I felt like a guest about to meet the royal court. I looked past Bernice to a crowd of people standing over a glass coffee table, lifting crackers and carrot sticks to their mouths. As Michael walked toward them, I had no choice but to follow, my arms like pendulums swinging from my shoulders. Robbed of my coat, my only protective prop, I felt naked, another layer removed.

"Hello, Michael!" A middle-aged man with a broad smile walked toward us, both arms outstretched. Thick white hair, stacked high atop his head, revealed streaks of black from his younger days. Bushy eyebrows fanned out over his eyes and lids. I liked him immediately. He was Einstein and Santa Claus all rolled into one.

"It's good to see you! How are you?" He smiled and chuckled, as if in the middle of a joke. His right hand clutched Michael's in a handshake, while his left patted his shoulder. I thought if I stood there and smiled one pace behind Michael, I just might be able to slip away into the kitchen to get a soft drink, or better yet, a glass of wine.

"And you must be Sally." I liked the way he said my name, stretching out the *a* and adding some nasal. It sounded like home.

"Honey, this is my Uncle Norman, my mom's brother."

I took his hand. "Hi, Norman. It's good to meet you."

"The pleasure is all mine." The way Uncle Norman leaned forward and looked into my eyes while holding my hand, I believed him. I immediately felt welcomed into his family. "I understand you're from Milwaukee. Your mayor is doing some wonderful things with welfare reform."

I looked at him, stunned. "How did you know I'm from Milwaukee? And about my mayor?"

"When I found out Michael was dating a beautiful woman and I was going to meet her, I had to do my research!"

He asked about the closing of various breweries and the

opening of the new art museum. With each question, the door opened wider for me to enter this family. I realized then that I wasn't only there to meet Michael's family. They were meeting me, and I was profoundly touched by his uncle's thoughtfulness.

Michael returned to my side, pressing his hand into the small of my back as he introduced me to the circle of people. There was Roberta, a jovial, round woman with flushed cheeks and cropped chestnut hair in tight curls. I imagined her home always smelled of chocolate chip cookies and pie. Dick, Roberta's husband and Bernice's cousin, stood next to his wife, his inverted-light-bulb body a complement to her perfect sphere. His short-sleeved white-cotton shirt pulled taut against a soft middle, and the generous bridge of his nose held up his rectangular wire-rimmed glasses. Light bounced off his nearly bald head. He nodded in my direction, smiled, and returned to his conversation.

Dick and Roberta's 20-year-old son, Eddie, was a surprise. His flawless dark skin and ink-black hair set him apart from the rest of us. I later found out they had adopted Eddie from South America as an infant. They had also adopted Eddie's sister, whom they later discovered was mentally challenged. She now lived in an assisted living facility and would not join us this Passover.

The circle of introductions continued. There was Bernice's cousin Louis, a paunchy, bearded man in his mid-thirties. Ira, his brother, resembled Dick and was married to Marsha, a nervous woman who pulled at her hangnails.

I tried hard to remember names but without much success. Instead I focused on relationships. Uncle Norman's wife was Joan, a tall, striking woman with soft brown eyes a shade lighter than her shoulder-length wavy hair. Their daughter, Karyn, a few years younger than me, reminded me of a boisterous Barbra Streisand. She leaned forward and talked rapidly, hand gestures emphasizing important points. It wasn't hard to get a handle on the rhythm of her banter.

"Where do you go to school, Karyn?"

"Baruch. I go to Baruch!"

"Is that down on 23rd Street?"

"Yes! 23rd and Lex." Her mousy brown curls bounced into her eyes and around her shoulders when she spoke. Her childlike enthusiasm endeared her to me. We stood side by side chatting, her hand often touching my forearm as we spoke. It was as if I had known her for years.

Karyn's brother Andy was the antithesis of his sister. Tall, with dark, cropped hair, Andy was reserved and pleasant in his speech. Judging by the fit of his jacket and the coordinating silk tie, there was no question Andy was a professional, and a successful one at that.

It seemed odd to be surrounded by people so eager to learn about me. I suddenly felt unqualified to talk about myself. Milwaukee? Well, I didn't know many facts about the city I grew up in. Having gone to two different colleges and studied overseas, it had been eight years since I had lived there. Fashion? I had just recently started my career on Seventh Avenue. I first worked in retail, then publishing, then taught aerobics before finally settling into my new job as a fashion merchandiser. I wasn't at all expert about the industry.

When I was young, the heat of the spotlight was as welcome as the hot sun at the beach. All through high school and college, I was the social coordinator, the practical jokester, and the Dear Abby to my friends, as well as a leader in several school organizations. If someone wanted to pull a prank on a fraternity, I was the one to mastermind a scheme. If a girlfriend was wrought with confusion over a boyfriend, she knew she could get some solid advice from me. When a club needed a new officer, I eagerly raised my hand.

As the years passed in New York, I slowly relinquished my role as center of attention. My fast-paced work environments offered little chance of connecting with co-workers, and my six roommates scattered every day and night. My hopes of bonding with Michael's friends faded like the fizz in an opened bottle of seltzer. Having tired of being talked over as if I had never spoken, I resigned myself to a new identity in his circle —that of the quiet one.

"Everyone! *Everyone!* Let's be seated!" Bernice's commanding voice called out from the end of the dining alcove. When we did not move instantly, she clapped her hands in a crisp staccato. "Okay, people. *People!* Let's sit down!"

Rectangular tables of irregular widths abutted one another, spilling into the living room a chair's depth from the sectional sofa. The table linens, although varying shades of white, blended well together. I glanced at the bottles of wine and the plates of crackers on the table and wondered, *What's the rush? The food isn't even set out yet.*

I pulled out a chair and stopped before seating myself. Everyone was standing, hands resting on the hard chair backs. At my family dinners, everyone strode to the table, yanked a chair away and plopped down. Our meter of manners was the timing of reaching for food: it would be bad manners to eat before joining in a blessing of the meal. If any of us made the blunder of grabbing for the gallon of milk or bowl of macaroni before our family prayer, we would hear my mother's admonishing voice singing out the criminal, "Have you forgotten something...?"

As Michael's family chatted with one another, I discreetly tucked my chair back under the table and surveyed the setting. There was virtually no food on the table. Large six-inch-square, pock-marked crackers stacked ten tall on plates were set at intervals along the length of table; between each were bowls of some sort of brown, nutty spread. Small butter dishes held a fuchsia dip of equally thick consistency sitting in a puddle of its own juice. Its splinter-like texture reminded me of the shards of the magnetic metal in tabletop sculptural games.

A dingy, gray, hardcover book, mottled with brown blotches and oil stains, was centered on each plate. The binding on my book was torn at the top. The flap splayed open, revealing the bark-like brown wrap and the mesh binding underneath. Black, squat Hebrew letters marched across the top of the book. Below the Hebrew words was an etching. At first I thought it was an abstract drawing until, upon closer observation, I saw it was a cloaked woman, hunched forward, carrying a basket the size of her body atop her head, laden with a leafy substance. Along the bottom border of the book, an inch above the worn, frayed edge, was the English translation: "The New Haggadah."

Bernice pushed through the swinging door of the kitchen, bringing with her the pungent waft of roast beef, potatoes and soup. I was surprised to see her enter empty-handed.

"Everyone. Sit down. Please."

I obeyed, squeezing my body into a chair between Michael and Karyn.

"Behold this cup of wine!" I turned to see Bernice sitting at the head of the table, glass held above her head. *What a strange way to start a prayer*, I thought, *or is it a toast?* A few people looked side to side, sneaking a peek at their neighbor's prayer book. I flashed back to third grade, peering over Shelly Peppy's shoulder so I could find my place in the textbook. Michael reached to his left to flip my book over in my hands. "You read Hebrew right to left."

Hebrew? I thought. *We were going to read Hebrew tonight?*

"Does everyone have a glass of wine?" Bernice sighed.

Hands reached for bottles amidst the exchange of polite murmurs. *Do you want red? You prefer white? I don't know if there is any water on the table. Maybe in the kitchen.*

"Behold this cup of wine!" Bernice started again, her voice even deeper and more theatrical the second time. "Let it be a symbol of our joy tonight as we celebrate the festival of *Pesach!*"

My eyes scanned the book for her words. Once I located the place where she read, my fingers slipped under the left page and flipped it over. Sure enough, there was a page of Hebrew, with the translation below it. Simple black-and-white illustrations of bearded men in yarmulkes and robes filled the margins. I flipped another page and found drawings of branches, with leaves fanning out from their length, and yet more Hebrew. Page 11 depicted a cloaked two-inch man with chained wrists held high in the air.

Everyone turned a page in unison.

"Praised be thou, O Lord our God, King of the Universe, who createst the fruit of the vine," Bernice continued.

Praised be thou? Createst? This was sounding a lot like mass. My stomach gurgled. I grabbed a dozen pages and curled them back. Certainly we couldn't read this entire book tonight. My eyes skimmed the lines, looking for the words Hanukkah or Yom Kippur, any evidence that the book was used for other holidays as well. Instead, I saw unpronounceable words like *afikomen, Paschal, Rabban Gamaliel* and *Gileadite.*

"Do we read this whole thing?" I dipped my shoulder toward Michael and whispered.

"Oh, no," he assured me. "We only read about half of it."

I turned to the end of the book. There were 175 pages.

"And we don't eat until we're finished reading?"

"We'll have some matzah soon." He pointed to the plate of flat crackers. I suddenly wished I had chosen two burritos for lunch in midtown over the modest tossed salad. I turned my book to the beginning, searching for the paragraph Bernice was reading.

"Praised be thou, O Lord our God, King of the Universe, who has enabled us to reach this season!" Bernice looked up from her Haggadah. "Now we drink our first cup of wine."

We all took a sip and set the crystal stemware down.

"Ira, your turn."

Turns? We would be taking turns reading? This was getting worse by the second. In school and in business meetings, I had always been the first to volunteer to read aloud. Classmates even told me I had a great reading voice. But tonight, reading from the Haggadah dotted with Hebrew words, I was a disoriented explorer ambivalently paddling a canoe.

Bernice ceremoniously held up a clump of parsley as if it were an artifact for all to admire. It was then that I noticed a platter in front of her displaying a dollop of the nutty spread, an egg, a bowl of water and a bone. I could only hope it wasn't a sampling of dinner. My stomach felt like a sinkhole.

"These greens are a symbol of the coming of spring," Ira intoned. "Before partaking in them, let us say together: 'Praised be thou, O Lord our God, who createst the fruit of the earth!'"

Ira paused, then nudged Marsha.

"This portion of the matzah is called the afikomen," Marsha squinted at the page. Bernice clasped a square cracker with two hands, held it above the table and snapped it in two. Norman brushed the spewed crumbs from his plate. "We shall share it in remembrance of the time when our ancestors would partake of the holiday sacrifice known as the Paschal lamb."

We were only six yellowed pages into the Haggadah and already I had no better grasp of what was going on than I had on page one. But I had no choice but to simply follow everyone else's lead. I scooped the nutty *harosset* onto the jagged fragment of matzah Michael handed me. I was suspicious of the lumpy brown mixture, the peculiar, chunky concoction reminding me of the tasteless food my mother used to set in front of us, a glob of something earthy and unrecognizable used to conceal a piece of chalky liver. But when the harosset hit my tongue, the tang of the nutmeg and apples and the crunch of the walnuts gave me hope. Here was something that satisfied my sweet tooth, moistened the dry cracker and satiated my hunger, if only for a little while.

As the 20 guests at the table took turns reading, we continued munching on matzah. It suddenly occurred to me that my turn was approaching. Realizing this, I regressed to elementary school student, counting the number of people ahead of me, matching them to paragraphs. The pronunciation of Jewish words frightened me, my heart rate intensifying at the thought of fumbling through a passage on my own. Until this night, I had never heard of matzah, harosset or Haggadah. Who knew what else lay ahead?

Michael sat to my right and read a long, easy paragraph. Mine looked to be the same.

"The rabbis of long ago used to love to tell and retell the story of Pesah," I said.

"*Pay-sahk*," a few people around the table corrected me.

My eyes darted to the side.

Karyn, sitting to my left, tutored me loudly. "It's *Pay-sahk*." My cheeks tingled with the embarrassment crawling up from my neck. "You need to get the *aahhk*."

Having never spoken a foreign language in my life, save a few words of Croatian my dad had taught me, I found myself at a disadvantage.

"Pes*ach*," I attempted. It was unnatural to gag my throat with the back of my tongue. I marched on.

"Once it happened that five rabbis became so interested in talking together about the freeing of the Israelites from Egypt, that they stayed up all night. There is a quaint tale told about these five rabbis."

I turned the page. My underarms moistened. Ahead of me were names that didn't look remotely familiar. I sucked my heart into my throat. If I couldn't handle Pesach, I didn't stand a chance of blundering my way through the next paragraph.

"Rabbi Eliezer and Rabbi Eleazar ben Azariah and Rabbi Akiba and Rabbi Tarfon...," Karyn chimed in. Processing my alarm had taken me so much time, it had disguised itself as a pause, and Karyn spared me humiliation. As she read, the elders at the table corrected Karyn's mispronunciations of the names. Karyn remained unaffected.

The cracking and crunching of matzah continued all around me as we recited the next 60 pages of the Haggadah. As I listened, resigned to the fact that I would be reading from a foreign text for at least an hour, I tried to extract some meaning from what I heard. What exactly was Passover about? There was a lot about an exodus from Egypt, the Jews being persecuted and fleeing for their lives. It was a piece of history I had known nothing about. While the story piqued my interest, I couldn't help but feel that this was the history of all the other people sitting around the table, not mine. The story of Passover simply did not resonate with me. My people, the Catholics, the Wisconsinites, the Croatians, had not grabbed for unleavened bread and made a run for it. We did not fight a pharaoh to win our right to practice our religion, at least not that I knew of. Over and over, the text referred to their tribe, imploring the reader to never give up their Jewish way of life, to always remember where they came from. I was fascinated, but I couldn't take ownership of the story. It was like paging through another family's photo album.

Yet the story of Easter had never held any meaning for me either. That Jesus was nailed to the cross until his death, only to be resurrected, was a story I had never quite believed. While I accepted that people were punished in this cruel fashion, it seemed mythological that he would then arise to save Christians. Plus, I never much cared for martyrdom. It was too self-serving.

Forty-five minutes passed as I tried to appease my stomach with matzah. I felt conspicuous eating almost an entire bowl of harosset myself, but no more conspicuous than Karyn reaching over my plate to snatch Michael's untouched wine. I started to fantasize about devouring a plate abundant with steaming beef and warm vegetables, the source of the enticing aroma from behind the swinging door. Would we ever abandon this Haggadah? Would I ever satiate my swelling appetite with a plateful of delectable food, leaving the dryness of the text behind?

"Die-die-ay-noo!" The room suddenly broke into song and clapping. "Die-die-ay-noo! Die-die-ay-noo! Dayenu, dayenu!"

The kitchen door swung open and Juanita entered, balancing four small plates on her forearms and palms. Bernice followed close behind with several more dishes. On each were oblong mounds of a firm oatmeal-like substance. I looked more closely at the plate set in front of me, touching my fingertip to the slimy surface. It was cold.

"*Gefilte* fish," Michael told me.

I gave him a blank stare.

"Ga-what fish?" I had dangled many a line into Wisconsin lakes. This was not fish.

"Put some horseradish on it." I was always willing to try something new, so I cut into the thick, ground-up fish and dipped it into the red mush Michael had spooned onto my plate. The chill muted the fish flavor and the tangy horseradish added the right amount of zest. To my surprise, I loved gefilte fish.

Before I could hope for seconds, the feast had begun. Wide-brimmed bowls of matzah ball soup were placed in front of us, a Jewish specialty that Michael and I enjoyed at the Second Avenue Deli on countless windswept afternoons. As delicious as the deli soup was, this was better. The salty chicken broth saturated the light, doughy dumplings, dissolving them on my tongue.

Bowls cleared, Juanita pushed through the door with a platter of beef brisket, and Bernice followed with roasted baby potatoes and carrots. Joan completed the line with two bowls of string beans littered with splinters of garlic.

"Juanita makes all of this?" I asked Michael

"Oh, no." He looked at me as if I should have known the answer. "My mother makes everything but the gefilte fish. Juanita just helps."

As the assortment of food increased, so did the volume of conversation. Sitting at the center of the activity, I could hear discussions at both ends of the table.

"Louis would know." Roberta leaned over Louis's plate toward Marsha. "He's a producer."

"Actually," quiet-spoken Louis held up a fork, "I'm a—"

"Well, maybe Louis doesn't know about *this* show," Marsha

challenged Roberta.

"I really don't produce, I—"

"Of course, he would know! He's a very big deal in television!"

"I work in develop—"

"A producer doesn't know about every show," Marsha insisted, dismissing her brother-in-law's interjections with a wave of her fork. Louis leaned back in his chair, resigned to his inaccurate job description.

All the while that debate went on, to my left, Andy and Karyn laughed, describing the childhood Seders at this very apartment.

"And this spot here!" Karyn pointed at her stained book. "This is where I spilled the matzah-ball soup!"

"Yeah, well I bet there's a new wine stain on your book after tonight," Michael teased.

Norman sparred with Ira over the state of the MENSA organization; Bernice made plans for her friends, Steve and Penny, to visit her in her house in the Hamptons; and Roberta fussed over Eddie's portions.

I was enchanted by it all. The contrast to the holiday dinners of my childhood was immense. At our table, we politely asked for dishes to be passed ("say 'please'") and my mother consistently reminded us not to fight at the table. Parents talked with one another about politics and current events, and children were told not to interrupt. Once we had eaten, we asked to be excused quickly so we could run back upstairs to play.

Here at the Seder table, I felt like a child again, surrounded by aunts, uncles and cousins. Yet, at this table, while the younger generation was still referred to as "the kids," we all had an equal voice. I wondered how Michael would have liked our Easter dinner. Would it be too quiet for him? Would the ham and potato salad seem alien? Our worlds seemed continents — and cultures — apart.

For hours at Seder we sat around the table, feasting on Bernice's cooking while enjoying seamless conversation. These family and friends gathered like this only once a year, yet spoke as if they coffee klatched every morning. People talked over one another, sometimes holding conversations from opposite ends of the table. After dinner and before dessert, guests engaged in an undeclared game of musical chairs, getting up from their seats to mingle with others who had been inaccessible. I relished the symphony of clanging dishes and clamorous conversation. By the time we carried gravy-smeared plates to the kitchen, I felt as if I had come home. It was precisely what I had wanted my childhood holidays to look, smell and sound like.

At the end of the evening, as we all stood and mingled near the front door, Michael warned me, "You're about to experience your first Jewish goodbye."

"Jewish goodbye?"

"It's when people say goodbye, but then talk for another hour," Michael explained. Sure enough, we ended up standing in the foyer with guests wearing their coats, congregating in clusters until I felt my swollen feet about to explode from my pumps.

After the last guest, we closed the door and I glanced into the dining room. I could still hear the laughter and banter filling the apartment, ghosts of guests who had left just moments before. I followed Michael to the kitchen, where he nibbled on shreds of brisket from a platter on the counter, while Bernice shuffled around the galley kitchen in her slippers, wrapping leftovers. As she asked Michael what he wanted to bring home, I envied him. How nice it would be to have a mom wrap up a meal of delicious food for me. I could imagine bringing home a package, taking a taste before going to bed that night and warming the food tomorrow for dinner. It would be like a college care package, a taste of home and a reminder of the people who loved me.

"Sally, is this enough brisket for you?" Bernice showed two paper plates with generous portions of every dish I had just eaten.

"That's perfect," I smiled, feeling loved to my core.

As we hugged and kissed goodbye at the door, Bernice's hand lingering on my cheek as she said, "Goodbye, dear," it occurred to me that I had found the type of extended family I had always envisioned.

Looking up at the gold, starburst-shaped clock hanging in the foyer, I noticed that the hands didn't move; time had stood still. It was precisely how I wanted life to be at that moment. Suddenly the apartment seemed strangely familiar. The silver-and-gray fleur-de-lis wallpaper, the red wooden figurines of Chinese men, the vase holding a cluster of 5-ft tall pussy willows. Perhaps it was less a feeling of familiarity and more an instinct that walking into this apartment would one day feel as comfortable as walking into my own home.

The door clicked behind us and we sauntered silently down the carpeted hall. I clasped Michael's fingers, the handle of my Bloomingdale's bag filled with leftovers dangling from my other hand. I hoped Bernice had packaged the love and unbridled energy of the evening with the foil-wrapped brisket, so that when I opened it I would experience the evening all over again.

I Do

I stood in the bar of the Wisconsin Club with my parents, gingerly dabbing the corners of my eyes with my fingertips.

"Barkeep, can we have a napkin for my daughter?" my father's voice boomed politely.

"You betcha."

"It's all right, Dad," I smiled, "I have a handkerchief in my sleeve." I touched the Venetian lace on the cuff of my wedding gown, feeling the satin-covered buttons.

"Is that the handkerchief from my grandmother?" my mother asked. She looked radiant in her full-length purple gown.

"Of course, Mom. It's my 'something borrowed'."

Layers of sentimentality trickled out in my tears, moments before I was to walk down the aisle. I felt very much like a girl again, and it seemed right that I would spend the last minutes of my single life with my parents. They had been divorced nearly twelve years, and I was moved, realizing it was the first time since childhood I had been alone in a room with both my mom and dad.

Next door, in the elegant Mitchell Room, a hundred people waited to hear me exchange my vows with the adoring, sophisticated, romantic man whom I loved more than I could imagine loving anyone. Even now, on my wedding day, I could hardly believe he loved me too.

The door opened and I glimpsed a cluster of men in tuxedos standing in the corridor outside, my future husband amongst them. Sonia, our wedding consultant, rushed in.

"Sally, we're late. Your guests are waiting."

"We're not starting until my brother-in-law gets here." Gonzalo, my sister's husband, had made a dash across town to drop off their baby with a sitter.

"But we're seven minutes late."

I heard the sound of melodious piano music playing next door and imagined my aunt's fingers dancing across the ivory keys. I was grateful that she had thought to fill the silence. Seated in the room were my Wisconsin aunts and uncles, my brothers and their wives, my New York friends, and Michael's family, from a collection of seven states, many of them having traveled across the country. I was certain that patience was not an issue for them.

"We're not in any hurry."

***

"I thought you weren't going to work late," Michael had said, a year earlier, as I sat at my desk a few feet from him, finishing up the day's reports at home.

"Don't worry," I said teasingly. "When we get married, I'll work less."

"Good." Michael smiled nervously as he reached for his sock and pulled out a palm-sized gray leather box.

"Michael..."

I looked at the box embossed with a jeweler's logo. Wariness, shock and giddiness swirled through me like an inverted tornado. This was the moment every woman anticipates, and I was unprepared, caught off guard.

"Open it."

I was stunned by a glistening round diamond perched high on a wide, gold band. The facets sparkled, winking tiny blue and pink circles of light into the room.

"Michael..."

The ring was so perfectly suited to my taste it seemed peculiarly familiar, as if I had always known it. In its simple and understated setting, I saw that Michael truly knew me.

"Michael… it's beautiful!"

"It was my grandmother's diamond. I reset it for you."

I had been told Bernice's mother had been a devoted parent, a published poet, a woman of great grace, who had died too early in her early forties. I had always felt a kindred spirit with her, imagining she and I would have loved each other's company. I could envision her diamond on my wrinkled hand 50 years from now, still sparkling as I held my grandchildren.

Michael clumsily stood and held my hand in his.

"Will you marry me?"

Tears sprang from my eyes. "Really?"

Michael laughed. "Yes, Sally. I really mean it. Will you marry me?"

The tornado dissolved, taking with it random thoughts of old boyfriends, of men who flirted with me still, of those I would never meet.

"Yes. I'll marry you."

We hugged and kissed and fell into each other's arms, cooing our disbelief and excitement.

"I have a couple of questions," Michael announced, disentangling himself.

"Yes?"

"Do you at any time want to move back to Wisconsin?"

"No," I answered, unequivocally, shocked at how quickly he could transform his romance into business. I had moved to New York just four years earlier and it already felt more suited to me than my home state.

"And I want to raise the kids Jewish. Is that a problem?"

I was taken aback. Aside from Passover and the High Holy Days, I had never seen Michael observe Judaism. He never attended Sabbath services, he could not tell me what the Hebrew

Hanukkah blessing meant, and took particular pleasure in decorating our Christmas tree every year.

"You want to raise our kids Jewish?"

"It's important to me."

Although I was surprised by Michael's stipulation, I had no religion to renounce in order to honor his wishes. When my parents divorced, our lifelong church friends had excluded our family from the holiday parties, Sunday brunches, and camping trips we had shared for 15 years. After that, I had released my ties to Catholicism and since then I had been actively seeking a new faith, looking for tenets that helped feed my spirituality. Learning about Judaism could be interesting. After all, Passover had been enjoyable, who knew what else I might discover? And no one was asking me to convert.

"Judaism won't be a problem," I assured him. "You can teach me what you know."

As we planned our wedding, differences in our background caused unexpected clashes. The first was about our wedding location.

"I can't get married in New York," I insisted to Michael. "None of my aunts or uncles will come if we have it here."

Not being a woman who had dreamed of her wedding since childhood, I had very few mental snapshots of my nuptials. But if I had any vague images, they were of dancing and celebrating with my family and friends, and I didn't think a Manhattan wedding, which by Michael's standards would be a black-tie affair, would lend itself to a roomful of people polkaing all night and toasting freely.

"I figured as much," Michael had answered. "Of course we'll have it in Wisconsin."

"Great!"

"We'll just have a black-tie wedding in Milwaukee."

"Um, I don't think there is such a thing."

"There are no black-tie weddings in Milwaukee?"

I cleared my throat. "Not in my family."

"Great! Then we'll be the first!"

Things seemed to be spiraling quickly. "Michael, if we dictate black tie, we may as well as have our wedding on Fifth Avenue, because my extended family won't come."

"We can't afford Fifth Avenue!"

I shrugged.

"Fine. We'll work around it." He thought for a moment. "We'll call it *Black Tie Invited*."

Deciding who would officiate at our wedding was our next obstacle.

"What are your feelings about a rabbi?" Michael fished, apprehensively.

"My feelings are I'll have no idea what a rabbi is talking about. Nor will my family."

The only Jewish wedding I had attended was that of Beth and David. I was amazed that much of the ceremony had been conducted in Hebrew. Although the rabbi had been a friend of theirs, making touching personal observations about Beth and David's relationship, it still bothered me that a lot of the service was spoken in a language the bride, groom and most of the guests didn't understand. I was reaching for something far more meaningful.

I also knew the point was moot. Even if I had agreed to have a rabbi officiate, it would involve an arduous search to find one who would marry a non-Jewish woman to a Jewish man, just as a Catholic priest would be unlikely to marry an interfaith couple. The only way a rabbi would conduct our ceremony was if I converted to Judaism, which was not an option for me.

"A rabbi is out of the question," I reiterated.

"Well, you *know* I won't get married by a priest."

"Of course not! I don't want to either."

As a little girl I had thought that my favorite priest, Father Joe, would one day conduct my wedding ceremony, but the idea had long ago been quashed. Not only were my ties to the Catholic Church nonexistent, the idea of a Jew getting married in the church seemed ludicrous. Listening to a priest repeatedly mention Jesus Christ, a given in a Catholic ceremony, would be alienating to Michael. Already Michael would be getting married in unfamiliar territory, in the Midwest culture that was not his own. I didn't want to make him feel any more out of place at his own wedding.

Another option, to be married by both a priest and a rabbi, seemed preposterous. It announced the couple's inability to make a compromise, a holding tight to their individuality. I believed marriage to be a partnership, a string of compromises made to form a future family. Trying to find two officials of two faiths seemed more an act of stubbornness than a fusion.

The truth was I had long ago relinquished the notion of a religious ceremony. While I loved the idea of being bound for life under one faith, I resigned myself to the fact that this was not to be for Michael and me. It was my one great sacrifice in our relationship—that we would not journey down the road of a shared faith, raising our children in a religion that was meaningful to both of us. As a result, I had no template for what our ceremony would look like. Eliminating the hour-long mass complete with homily and communion, traditional in Catholicism, as well as a Jewish service, of which I would understand little, I figured we would be creating a service of our own design, one that blended our two cultures.

So, one day while visiting Milwaukee, we stopped at a corner pay phone and called a local judge. Two phone calls later we locked into Judge DiMotto, a nice Italian man with a strong Midwest accent.

No sooner was the judge engaged than Michael surprised me with yet another hurdle.

"My mom really wants us to get married after sundown," Michael told me as we pored over sample wedding invitations.

I looked up from my wedding-planning binder.

"Sundown? That's at 7 o'clock! We'll hardly have a wedding day!"

In Catholic weddings, the ceremonies start in the late morning or early afternoon, followed by pictures of the wedding party at different locations, then the reception and dinner. I had loved the idea of spending all day in my gown, surrounded by my friends and family for private picture time before joining the dinner and dancing portion of the evening.

"Why after sundown?"

"That's when the Sabbath ends."

"Sabbath ends?" I asked, incredulously. "Since when do you observe the Sabbath?"

"Uh, we don't." Michael scratched his ankle. "But you know, it's tradition."

"Well, did you tell your mother we're not having a Jewish wedding?"

"I know, I know…she just mentioned it."

I wanted a close relationship with Bernice and it was important to me that we include her in our wedding plans. She and I shopped together for my wedding dress and for her mother-of-the-groom gown. We asked her to select our table wine, and she planned the entire menu for the rehearsal dinner she would host. The last thing I wanted to do was alienate my future mother-in-law, so Michael and I settled on a 6 pm ceremony, twilight. We would take pictures beforehand, thereby lengthening our day.

***

Now, as I stood in the small bar of the private club, blotting my tears with the corner of my great-grandmother's lace handkerchief, I was glad that the hard black-and-white differences in background blended into a soft, comforting, dappled gray. Our wedding would be held in the exclusive Wisconsin Club, an historic venue in downtown Milwaukee. A turn-of-the-century mansion with elaborate hand-carved mahogany woodwork, paneled walls and ornate fireplaces, it was a venue that reflected our style and taste.

Sonia rushed into the bar.

"Gonzalo is here."

I took a sharp breath and looked at each of my parents.

"Okay." I tucked my handkerchief back into my sleeve. "I'm ready," I said as the muted sound of cello, piano and violin drifted from the other side of the imposing oak door, Pachelbel's Canon in D played by my aunt and two nieces. I imagined the groomsmen walking down the aisle two by two followed by Michael and Bernice and my bridesmaids.

"Okay, you can come out now." Sonia swung open the door as the tangerine chiffon dress of the last bridesmaid turned the corner to enter the Mitchell room.

I grasped the crook of my father's elbow and felt the light touch of my mother's hand on my arm. The music paused and a Mozart movement began.

I had posed for family photos in the Mitchell Room just hours earlier; now the ambience had shifted from a bright photographer's site into a luminous, romantic setting. The dimmed crystal chandeliers, fused with the setting sun, cast sienna warmth in the room as if reflecting the glow of a fireplace. The wall of exterior French doors, draped in chiffon, filtered parcels of light through the panes, softly illuminating the floral topiaries on the pedestals flanking the length of the aisle.

Looking to the satin runner lined by swags of crinoline suspended between the white pedestals, I took in the rows and rows of guests. I had been warned it would be difficult to remember to smile as I walked down the aisle. But my problem was trying to contain my emotion. With each step I took, I was struck by how full my world was and how fortunate I was to have so much love in my life.

As I walked down the runner, all heads turned and I was welcomed by an array of smiling faces. Glimpsing Uncle Peter and Aunt Ginger, my youngest, 'cool' aunt and uncle, I flashed back to being a preadolescent sitting cross-legged on the floor of their bedroom, mesmerized by the pressed flowers and love letters Aunt Ginger showed me in her wedding scrapbook. Aunt Nancy and Uncle Larry beamed and I saw myself running on a grassy slope on their farm upstate, playing with my cousins at a family reunion. I passed Ann, an old friend from Milwaukee, whom I remembered meeting at a DECA Club conference in high school. My walk down the aisle became a walk through my life, passing all the people who formed me and all the points that led me to Michael.

As we neared the platform, my eyes rose to where Michael stood, hands clasped in front, smiling broadly. I hugged my parents, then stepped up to stand beside my future husband, who reached for my hand. I felt at home.

"Hi," Michael whispered.

Judge DiMotto nodded to us.

"Dear Sally and Michael. Today you are surrounded by your family and friends, all of whom are gathered to witness your marriage and to share in the joy of this occasion, which is one of the most memorable and happy days of your life."

Before I knew it, Judge DiMotto was introducing Beth, Debbie and Nicky, who each read a poem Michael and I had selected. It was a welcome departure from the Catholic weddings I attended, at which I had only heard readings from scriptures. Everything about our ceremony reflected who we were.

Debbie left the foot of the bema, teary eyed after reading her poem, and Judge DiMotto continued.

"It is in the Jewish tradition that Sally and Michael stand under a *huppa* as they exchange their vows. The openness of this huppa pledges that there will be no secrets. Family and friends stand at the corners, weighing the fragile structure down."

When I had stepped onto the platform under the huppa, I had immediately felt I was stepping into a sacred space. Four posts wrapped in white satin anchored the corners of a 10-ft by 10-ft square, each timber holding up yards and yards of draped crinoline that formed a translucent canopy above us. Standing under the huppa, flanking Michael in the center, were our closest friends and my sisters.

The judge continued, "The flimsiness of the huppa reminds us that the only thing that is real about a home is the people in it who love and choose to be together. The only anchors they will have will be each other. It is a house of promises. It is a home of hope."

The idea that a huppa represents the house had made sense to me when I researched it, but it wasn't until I stood under the shelter that life was breathed into the tradition.

Beside me stood Chrissy, my sister who had become my best friend; my sister Margie; and three college girlfriends. Behind Michael were his groomsmen, college friends who were like brothers, all smiling brightly. The heat of love and deep affection swaddled us beneath the fabric and flowers.

The intimacy I felt under the huppa was very different from feelings I'd had at the church alter the few times I'd stood as a bridesmaid. There, sharing the open space of the sanctuary, my role was as a witness to the marriage. God was proclaimed to be the source of strength and guidance for the newly married couple. I liked that Judaism declares loved ones to be the source of counsel and wisdom for the married couple, in addition to God. Sharing the protective space of the huppa with our wedding attendants symbolized this belief.

These were the friends and siblings with whom we would celebrate the birth of our children and mourn the death of our parents. Standing under the huppa together, I was reminded that we could no more be sheltered from the surprises of life than the fabric could protect us from storms. But the people who stood under the huppa with us gave us a strong foundation from which to launch into married life. I would not be going it alone with Michael.

It was common to have the parents of the bride and groom stand under the huppa as well. I would have liked my dad, mom and Bernice to join us there, but I thought my father would be uncomfortable practicing a Jewish custom. So we decided to follow the Catholic custom of our parents being seated in the first row.

"In the Catholic tradition, it is customary to exchange the sign of peace when we greet one another through handshakes and embraces," Judge DiMotto continued. "We all want peace in the world, and we know that peace begins in the hearts of each of us. In this tradition, you may now offer your friends and family and all those around you the Sign of Peace."

At every mass I attended, as well as every wedding, congregants shared the Sign of Peace, a moment when they shook hands or gave a fond embrace. I always liked this time of connection as well as the reprieve from the standing-sitting-kneeling ritual of mass.

I thought bringing this tradition to my wedding would be a nice way to make my family feel comfortable in an otherwise foreign ceremony. I had been the only person among my dozens of extended family members to be married by a justice of the peace in a nonreligious ceremony outside of a church, at dusk, black tie optional. Making my family feel at ease was important to me.

As Michael and I hugged and kissed our attendants, I looked to see Nicky and Beth nervously giggle as they limply shook hands with one another; Debbie and her fiancé, Steven, hugged; and David, Beth's husband, shook the hands of other New Yorkers behind him. Beyond them, my aunts and uncles reached across the aisle and turned to rows around them, warmly saying hello and hugging. As my aunt and my cousins played a folk song, Michael and I stepped off the platform and embraced our parents and my grandparents. I could see it was awkward for our Jewish friends, but just as my family learned something about the traditions I was marrying into, so Michael's family and our New York contingent was learning about me.

Since being a young girl attending scores of Catholic nuptials the length of a one-hour mass, I knew one day I would want a much shorter service for my own wedding. It seemed more romantic to focus the ceremony on the magnitude of marriage and the anticipation of unknown joys and trials. Deciding against a religious ceremony allowed me to have the short service I had envisioned.

"Repeat after me," Judge DiMotto recited, "In token and pledge of the vow between us made, with this ring, I do thee wed."

Michael relaxed now, and his voice carried confidently.

"In token and pledge of the vow between us made, with this ring, I do thee wed."

After we exchanged rings, we had one more custom to enact before returning down the aisle.

"A tradition of the Jewish religion is the stepping on the glass by the groom after exchanging vows," boomed Judge DiMotto, holding up a napkin wrapped tightly around a wine goblet, then setting it on the floor in front of Michael. "The glass is broken to protect the marriage. As this glass shatters, so may your marriage never break."

The judge looked up to address the guests directly. "When the glass is broken, it is customary to yell, '*Mazel tov!*' — a Jewish phrase expressing congratulations and meaning *good luck.*"

Michael bent his right knee, raised his leg and smashed his heel onto the napkin. As I heard the shattering of glass under his shoe, I was more startled at the sound of a rousing "Mazel tov!" yelled in unison throughout the room. Never could I have imagined the impact of having my Catholic friends and family calling out a Hebrew blessing in unison. While everything Jewish had seemed so foreign to me, my family seemed quite comfortable shouting their first Hebrew phrase, as if they had shouted it at countless celebrations. If my aunts, uncles, cousins and friends, all completely unknowledgeable about Judaism until this day, could call out a blessing with such exuberance, who knew what was possible for me?

"By the virtue of the power vested in me by the State of Wisconsin, I now pronounce you husband and wife. You may kiss the bride."

With that one kiss, any bit of anxiety I had had about my future in a New York Jewish world had been relinquished. I could see now that to live a New York Jewish life, I wouldn't have to sacrifice anything. My Midwestern Catholic family had stepped into Jewish traditions with total acceptance. My New York Jewish friends thought nothing of coming to Wisconsin to be at our wedding. For the first time, it seemed possible that perhaps I could embrace Judaism as my own one day.

The First High Holy Days

"It really would be nice, dear, if you would join us for the High Holy Days."

We sat on Bernice's plush amber sectional in her Upper East Side apartment, enjoying a glass of wine before dinner. The chocolate-brown living room walls set off her collection of artwork, the color both elegant and unpredictable, a reflection of the woman who lived there.

I plastered a smile on my face and raised my eyebrows, an automatic response I used in uncomfortable situations. Every autumn, when Michael took a sick day from work, donned a suit and went to synagogue with his mother, his only description of Rosh Hashanah and Yom Kippur services was "long." Of course I had never volunteered to go. Now, within my first year of marriage, my grace period had ended. Michael's mother had just invited me to temple.

I quickly considered the possible repercussions of declining the invitation. Michael and I had been married just five months, and I had agreed to raise our children Jewish. Although far from starting a family, if I refused the invitation to attend synagogue, I might appear to have been in bad faith, not really interested in Michael's religion.

For the three years that Michael and I had been together, Michael had been enjoying the perks of dating and marrying a Catholic girl — most of them revolving around Christmas. He loved playing the collection of contemporary Christmas music he started, ranging from top-40 artists like Madonna to jazz greats like Count Basie and Lou Rawls. He devoured my homemade Christmas snickerdoodles and my sister Chrissy's annual care package of Christmas cookies as well. But, most of all, he loved Christmas trees.

"It's a whole new way of expressing myself," he beamed, standing in a forest of decorated evergreens on the fifth floor of Macy's. "Let's have a theme tree this year. How about these? These Christmas ducks are cute!"

We later learned that the "ducks" were, in fact, representative of the traditional Christmas goose. But Michael loved our "ducks" just the same, and established a new tradition of a fowl-themed tree.

Ever since we had moved into our first apartment together two years earlier, we had purchased our tree from a corner tree lot, dragging it home through the snow and maneuvering it into the elevator to our floor. We hosted Christmas parties, Michael greeting our guests with gusto, offering them their choice of wine or eggnog, stacking his assortment of Christmas CDs to rotate throughout the night. The only caveat Michael had in celebrating Christmas was forbidding a wreath on our apartment door. "It would advertise that we have a Christian home, and we don't."

So I felt it was important that I, in turn, show an active interest in Michael's predominant holiday — the High Holy Days. Plus there was another level of concern in my decision about attending temple. If I didn't accept my first invitation to synagogue, I would also risk insulting my mother-in-law, for whom I had great respect. Michael was Bernice's only son. I was sure that before Michael proposed to me, she carried an image of her future daughter-in-law as a nice Jewish girl. Yet she never treated me as something less than she had expected. Bernice had welcomed me into her family, not just as her son's wife, but as a daughter.

"Okay..." I feigned a smile. "It'll be nice." I anticipated having to sit through an unfamiliar service for hours, where not only the rituals would be incomprehensible but the language as well. I knew what to expect in the hour-long Catholic mass. The entrance of the priest, the greetings, blessing of the holy water, the readings, the homily, communion, closing liturgies and the exit. The predictability was comforting. But I couldn't imagine what would fill three hours in synagogue. Would there be a lot of singing? Would we sit for long periods of time in silent prayer? Would I feel awkward, standing when I should sit? Would there be preaching of Jewish doctrines I wouldn't understand, having no frame of reference?

"Wonderful," Bernice said. "Now we just have to figure out the tickets."

"Tickets? You need to get tickets for the service?"

"Not *get* tickets, dear. *Buy* tickets. Let's see, I have to buy Michael's ticket..." She gazed across the apartment, calculating the expense.

"Wait a minute. The temple makes you buy tickets for a service you're required to attend?"

"No, dear..."

I was relieved to hear it. How could a religious organization charge admission?

"...not if you're a member, which, of course, I am. They only charge for guests." She looked at me as if to say, "Of course, the left shoe goes on the left foot."

"How much do they charge?"

"I think its 85 dollars this year."

"Eighty-five dollars!" I had never heard of anything so ludicrous. It would be like charging people to go to midnight mass. Was this a New York thing? In the spirit of theater, charging people to experience the spiritual spectacle of Rosh Hashanah?

Michael jumped in, ready to defend his customs. "Well, we don't pass a plate every Sunday to collect money. We pay a membership so we —"

"You have to *pay* to belong to a synagogue?" This just did not seem spiritual. It seemed mercenary. Houses of worship should welcome everyone, without questions.

All around New York I passed churches whose doors remained open throughout the day. I sometimes climbed their steps to steal a few moments of solitude away from the hectic pace of the city. And I felt welcome walking into any church, as if arms draped in white robes reached across the threshold and guided me into the sanctuary.

Judaism deeply offended me with their concept of exclusivity. Were synagogue doors closed and locked to outsiders? I hoped my astonishment would expose the sham of an admission fee for what it was.

"Maybe if Michael goes in first with me, I could come back out with *his* ticket and give it to Sally." Bernice was never easily sidetracked.

I sighed. With the conversation advancing from the temple charging admission to my mother-in-law conniving to sneak me in to services, I got up to go to the bathroom. I wondered why this was the religion in which Michael so wanted to raise his children.

Since I could remember, God's presence was palpable in my life. The wind blew and God waved hello with the swaying branches of trees. The Divine blessed me with rains when I needed to slow down the pace of life, luring me to stay inside with a good book or with close friends. God showed me the joy of life with the laughter erupting between friends. I wanted a religious community that embraced God's simple and direct love. Now, feeling that Michael thought one attends the High Holy Days out of servitude rather than to seek something more meaningful, I couldn't help but wonder if we were mismatched.

***

As we approached Central Synagogue on East 55th Street near Park Avenue, uneasiness seeped in, beginning with a tingling on my skin and penetrating to my stomach. What would I experience on the other side of the paneled walnut doors? Would I look conspicuous? I had carefully selected a conservative tweed skirt and jacket. A wonderful perk of working on Seventh Avenue was the free wardrobe and the confidence that I always had the appropriate outfit in my closet. But would the bewilderment in my eyes betray me, exposing me for the outsider that I was?

I gazed up at the Moorish architecture of the synagogue. Three sets of immense double doors stood squat between two towers. Layers of thick bricks in multiple shades of brown and beige were stacked high to create the bastion-like exterior. A sense of history oozed from the mortar. Trepidation about my first experience in a synagogue descended on me like a heavy fog. Suddenly it seemed like there was a great deal at stake. If I didn't like what I heard today, how could I raise our kids Jewish? Would I destroy my relationship with the man I loved if I couldn't embrace, or even respect, his religion?

"What will I do in temple?" I asked Michael.

"Just do what I do. But first, look at what all the people are wearing." He smiled. "I hope we get the balcony. I can get a really good view from up there."

I knew Michael was joking. At the same time, I understood that there was an element of truth in his words, though I couldn't fault him. It's not as if I had ever gleaned anything terribly meaningful from the hundreds of masses I had attended as a child. Sitting in a pew week after week, enduring my brother's pokes in the arm and my parents' shushes, my mind wandered at every service. Would Father Kleifish fall asleep at the altar? Was Mrs Struzyinski's butt so wide and flat from decades of sitting on pews? Certainly the colorful New York crowd would be even more entertaining to observe.

"Hellloooo!" Bernice sang out to us from the base of the steps, waving tickets above her head. We hugged and she handed me a ticket.

"Do I have to get this back to Michael?" I whispered.

"No, dear." She squeezed my hands in her gloved fingertips. "This one is for you." The affection in her eyes sent heat through my chest like hot chocolate after an afternoon of tromping through the snow. With the simple act of handing me a ticket, my mother-in-law validated me as an attendee of the services and as a member of her family. My hand on the crook of her arm, we ascended the graceful stairs of the synagogue.

As soon as I walked through the front doors, I was transported back to the ornate churches and cathedrals I had become entranced with while backpacking around Europe six years earlier. Sitting in a pew as the filtered light from the stained glass windows cast a glow over the church, I always felt renewed and at peace. I loved entering churches, leaving the frenetic outside world behind me. I'd sit upright in a pew and close my eyes, inhaling the smell of burning candles, the dim lights offering my eyes and soul precious moments of calm. Often the pews had padded seats that emitted a musk from years of dust. But more than anything, it was the stillness I was drawn to. I could meditate and reflect in peace. Neither the muted echoes of footsteps nor the hushed whispers of other visitors disturbed me.

I later took an architecture course at my university in London. It was there that I learned that the feeling of reverence religious architecture evokes is not a fluke. Spires straining toward the sky make us feel as if we are reaching towards the heavens. The altar elevates the priest or minister a tier above the churchgoers and a step closer to God. Stained glass windows depict portions of the Bible but also shut out the outside world, enclosing the church-goers in a haven of holiness. I had been saddened that the church I was raised in had little architectural interest. Built in the 1950s, Our Lady of Lourdes consisted of a series of squat rectangular boxes adjoining one another. The ceiling height was modest, and what few stained glass windows there were contained contemporary lines, sacrificing a sense of history.

Crossing the threshold from the lobby into the sanctuary of Central Synagogue, I was stopped short, dazzled by colors like I'd never seen in a church. Gilded, carved beams vaulted several stories above my head, crossing one another to create recessed squares on the ceiling. In each section, small, yellow, hand-painted stars of David shined against a vibrant, deep-blue background. Below, stained glass windows, each several stories tall, cast more luminous stars onto the sanctuary. The temple gleamed with holiness.

I was comforted by the symmetry of the sanctuary. The main floor was divided into four sections. The center aisle sliced a cube of seating into rows that sat approximately ten people each. Bordering each of those was another aisle and outer sections. Gothic columns supported two balconies that flanked the sanctuary. The columns framed perfectly curved arches, where glistening chandeliers hung like inverted wedding cakes.

I hadn't expected to see pews. I thought this uncomfortable manner of sitting was exclusively Catholic. While disappointed that I was back in the land of hard seating, I was also encouraged. *It's not that unlike a church*, I thought to myself.

"Let's go upstairs." Michael pressed a hand on my back. We climbed the stairs to the balcony and took seats overlooking the masses of people congregating below us. I noticed we were sitting in padded chairs.

I peered over the railing and turned to Michael, "What are people doing down there?" I asked, gazing at the throng of people standing, mingling and talking. At Our Lady of Lourdes, we would press one knee to the floor before entering a pew, then seat ourselves quietly, discreetly glancing around to see who else had arrived. The scene below me was startling. People talked at street volume, as if they were chatting at the intermission of the opera or a play. Coats were strewn across the length of pews to reserve seating, while congregants held post, standing in their rows, their backs turned to the front of the sanctuary. Men and women waved to others entering, and clusters of teenagers congregated in the aisles. While everyone dressed in what I would call their "Sunday best," there was no air of formality in their behavior.

"The organ is over there," Michael pointed to our left. A loft anchored the rear of the synagogue, its three walls covered with organ pipes of graduating heights. They dipped at the center of the back wall, framing yet another stained glass medallion. An organ rested in front of the display, diminished by the massive pipes.

"It's from the 1800s."

"Wow. No kidding,"

"This is the oldest temple in New York. Probably one of the oldest in the country."

I had no idea Michael felt such pride in his synagogue. While my childhood church found its way into many of our conversations, Michael never mentioned his temple, the rabbis, or anything temple-related for that matter. I thought the synagogue played little importance in his life. Another layer of Michael started to reveal itself.

"And that over there is the bema."

My eyes turned to what I call the altar.

"This is strange for me."

"What is?"

"There is no crucifix."

Of course I had known that there would not be a Jesus hanging from a cross and towering ominously above an altar. But to experience its absence was more unsettling than I would have expected. What was I supposed to look at during services? At Our Lady of Lourdes, I had memorized every crevice and crease in our carved Jesus' hair and loincloth. I remember vividly the woeful look in his half-closed eyes cast downward at us. I had spent hours of my childhood wondering if he was looking at me, pitting the logic of that impossibility against the illusion. Now, here I sat in the sanctuary of my dreams, feeling terribly out of place without a familiar religious emblem as my anchor.

Michael talked a little more about the temple, explaining how the prayer book is read from the right side rather than the left, but my eyes kept darting to the empty space above the pulpit.

The organ played and I watched people scurry to their seats. I was glad to see they took the entrance of their rabbi more seriously than they took the sanctity of the synagogue. But as the rabbi strode down the aisle clutching a book across his chest, I noticed something strange. A procession of about eight people followed him, and they clearly were not part of the clergy. Upon closer inspection, I saw that there were several clergy walking together to the bema. All three wore full-length white cloaks, with fringed shawls draping around their necks and falling past their waistlines. I assumed the elderly man with the widest and largest shawl, or *tallit*, was the senior rabbi, the others assistant rabbis.

But who was the group following them? Dressed in crisp suits and tailored dresses like all the other congregants in the synagogue, several wearing tallits draped around their necks, none even closely resembled the clergy. Yet they all headed straight to the bema, plopping themselves down in the cushy armchairs as if they belonged there. Didn't they know that the step up on the platform was one step closer to God, reserved for holy people?

"Who are those people?" I whispered and nodded to the front of the sanctuary.

Michael looked to the bema and shrugged. "Just people who belong to the temple."

"Why are they up there?"

He squinted with a smile, as if offered a brainteaser. "I don't know."

"Do they stay up there the whole time?"

"Yes. Shhh. The cantor is going to sing."

My eyes fixed on the middle-aged man at the bema — one of

the clergy I had mistaken for an assistant rabbi. I sat waiting for him to announce the hymn. When I attended mass every Sunday as a child, including many a guitar mass in the 1970s, the congregation always turned to the specified page number in our songbooks, then sang along with the person leading us.

But nobody turned a page of a hymnal. Instead, the cantor opened his mouth, and began delivering a solo. In Hebrew. Yet as soon as I began to despair about the long hours ahead of me, I found myself becoming lost in the melodic strains of what sounded like an aria. Like no music I had ever heard in any church, this was more like what I heard at the Metropolitan Opera. I closed my eyes and became lost in the experience.

"Will he ever sing in English?" I asked once the cantor sat back down. My shoulder touched Michael's as I leaned into him. He shook his head.

"Do you understand what he's singing?"

"Not really."

I'm sure my eyes gave an exaggerated "this-is-crazy" look. Even though the cantor's voice made me think of Luciano Pavarotti, if Michael didn't know what he was singing, where was the meaning? I was used to belting out verses that declared the congregation's reverence for God. Singing favorite hymns such as "We gather together to ask the Lord's blessing; He chastens and hastens His will to make known" not only broke the monotony of ritualistic standing, kneeling and sitting, and allowed us to stretch our vocal chords after long periods of silence, but singing our lyrical praises in unison gave us the feeling of unity with everyone in the church.

As the service continued, I paged through the prayer book. As in the Catholic Church, the service consisted of a lot of standing up and sitting down, although there was no kneeling, for which I was glad. When I tried to follow the prayer book, I saw that about 40 percent of the service was written in English, so I had little chance of following along. How I would survive more than two hours?

But while the text escaped me, the rituals captivated me. When the rabbi opened the ark, the tall armoire-like cabinet on the bema, the congregation stood and bowed.

"That's the Torah," Michael explained.

Two heavy 3-ft scrolls were lifted out of the ark and held high by the wooden poles protruding from the bottom. A cloth covering was removed and various congregants sang Hebrew passages from the scrolls. I later learned that each letter of the Hebrew alphabet is also a note, so while reading the Torah, the verses are also sung.

The chanting was mesmerizing. Looking down in my prayer book at the strange-looking language, I couldn't imagine learning how to read Hebrew, comprehend its meaning and even sing it.

Baruch atah Adonai, Elohaynu, melech ha-olam asher keed'shanu b'meetzvotav v'tzeevanu l'had'lik neir shel yom tov.

I felt like I was living in history. Although I didn't comprehend a syllable of the language, it struck me that all around me, in contemporary New York City, people chanted the original language of the Bible. With every word they were keeping their heritage alive. In fact, on this holy day, Jewish people all over the world were chanting the same ancient text.

The cantor approached the bema. "The great *shofar* is sounded. A still, small voice is heard. This day, even the angels are alarmed, seized with fear and trembling as they declare: 'The Day of Judgment is here!'"

"You'll like this." Bernice leaned across Michael and touched my arm. "It's to wake us up and bring us into the New Year."

I watched as a man strode to the bema, held a 4-ft curved ram's horn to his mouth and blasted air through its narrow passage. Its majestic battle cry, rough and static, sounded like a trumpet calling a cavalry to arms. As a former French horn player, I was impressed that the shofar player could force anything resembling a musical sound from this ancient instrument. The rabbi answered each blast with an equally loud Hebrew chant, "Tehiyahhhh!" Bernice was right. It had definitely succeeded in getting my attention.

After the drama of the shofar, the service settled back down, with me following the best I could, the whole time wondering if I could ever get used to a synagogue. In time I could adjust to the lack of crucifix. It no longer held a deep, spiritual meaning to me. I never had been comfortable with the idea that God placed an intermediary between Himself and His people. I had always prayed directly to God. I meant no offense to His son, if indeed He had one. So I could imagine one day becoming at ease with the absence of the crucifix, which would symbolize a separation from my childhood relationship with my family and the embracing of my next phase in life.

But there was the problem of the language. It seemed so foreign. I knew it would take time to adjust to all of the Hebrew, both spoken and sung. But, who knows? Maybe I would actually learn Hebrew one day. I had already adjusted to being silent when the cantor chanted. With no singing expected of me, a meditative trance engulfed me when he was up at the bema. It was enchanting, listening to such an old language being spoken by hundreds of congregants. I felt as if I had traveled far across distant lands and had come upon a house of worship where time had stood still. It was as if ancient traditions were upheld in this place, connecting the past and the present, and it comforted me.

While I missed singing along with hymns, I certainly could get used to hearing the beautiful melodies sung in unison by others.

Although few joined the cantor in the first song, much of the congregation raised their voices in unison for most of the other melodies. Looking around me, I could see that they were typical New Yorkers, transformed when they opened their mouths. Who would guess, as I passed them every day on the street, that they could sing and speak Hebrew?

It suddenly seemed that New York was filled with secret spiritual beings, people with histories and heritages. There was an exotic world that went on behind the doors of a synagogue, and it was a culture that could open up for me. My curiosity about Judaism was piqued. What was it liked to be raised Jewish? To have matzah ball soup served at dinner? To have grandparents that spoke Yiddish? To sing in Hebrew? What was it like to belong to a heritage so old, so rich in tradition?

"This is the sermon," Michael whispered to me.

Ahhh, I thought. *This I'm used to.* I had always loved sermons as a child. They gave me perspective in life in the chaotic household I grew up in. The priest's words always inspired me to rise above the pettiness of siblings tattling or playing with my toys without permission. I sat through Sunday after Sunday of meaningless ritual because my mother required it. But I listened to the sermon because I wanted to.

I settled back in my seat, glad for the cushion. We had been alternately sitting and standing for two hours. Now would be the payoff. I was ready for a lesson on life.

The rabbi stood at the pulpit and pulled on his tallit with one hand, bringing it closer to the sides of his neck. I saw in his thinning gray hair and his slightly stooped demeanor not his age but his wisdom. He tapped a few sheets of paper on end between his fingers, brought them into a neat stack and set them on the stand.

"*L'shana tova.*"

"L'shana tova," the congregation answered in unison.

"We are here as parents, as brothers, as sisters, as friends. We are here as one to celebrate and bring in our New Year. We are here as Jews."

Prayer books snapped closed around me as people adjusted themselves in their seats.

"As it is every Rosh Hashanah, I see many faces here today

that I do not see throughout the year."

I grinned. I *knew* there had to be more to being a Jew than going to temple once a year. I silently told them all *I told you so* while the rabbi gave them all a proverbial slap on the wrist.

"Yet, be not mistaken, you are here today for one reason. Because you are Jewish. Because being Jewish is important to you."

He paused and looked around the synagogue. I felt immediately we were of identical thinking. Attend services. Become part of a community. Show up for what you believe in.

"But our numbers are dwindling!"

Numbers are dwindling? I thought. I saw a few people leave the sanctuary before the sermon, but I assumed they were going to the bathroom.

"Our children are intermarrying. We are losing Jews!"

Losing Jews? I thought. *You were just about to gain one!*

I fixed my eyes on the rabbi and they hardened. My breath heaved unevenly in my chest, my ordinary reaction to anger and self-consciousness. "With every interfaith marriage, Judaism is at stake."

I imagined a hundred grimacing faces staring down at me, their bodies half-standing out of their seats. I saw their hands clutching jagged rocks, their arms cocked over their heads. I wanted to duck, preparing to dodge stones that would soon be hurled at me. I would be their token criminal, the outsider trying to disassemble their tribe, stealing away their Jewish young man.

The rabbi went on to support his claims with statistics. Jews who marry outside their faith seemingly had a low rate of observance. Interfaith marriages typically raise their children as Christians, or worse yet, with no religion at all. As the rabbi spoke, I wanted to yell out, "Hey, I agreed to raise the kids Jewish. I'm here! At least I'm trying!"

Michael shifted in his seat. I felt Bernice's discomfort next to him. This was the quietest the sanctuary had been during the entire two-hour service. The only sounds were the rabbi's booming voice and the occasional cough from the pews.

I hoped the rabbi would segue into another topic. Maybe he would describe the need to support Israel, for instance.

"Do not wait for your children to meet their future spouses at college or in the workplace. It is your obligation as Jews to create opportunities for them to meet other young Jewish adults. Talk with one another! Know each other's children! Introduce your children to other Jews. We must keep the Jewish faith alive!"

My jaw clenched. This man did not know me. Who was he to tell Michael that he made a mistake by marrying me? We shopped together, confided in one another our painful memories and our dreams for the future. We held hands while reading books in bed. My heart skipped a beat every time he called from work, which was about six times a day. Were we to believe our love was undesirable because I wasn't Jewish?

I closed my ears to the rabbi's voice, slamming shut the door to Judaism and dead-bolting the lock. I did not want entry to this religion. I did not even want to glimpse it down the hall. They wanted to keep themselves separate from the outside world. It suddenly seemed nothing more than a snobbish, exclusive club. I didn't believe Michael or his family felt this way. But if their religion did, I wanted no part of it. Michael was welcome to raise our not-yet-conceived children Jewish. I vowed that he would do it on his own.

Judaism 101

Michael and I zipped across Central Park in a cab after work, the trees and pedestrians a blur as the cab driver tailgated the car ahead of us.

"I really don't want to be late for our first class." I leaned forward as if trying telepathically to control traffic through the windshield.

Judaism 101 was scheduled to begin in 15 minutes, and the cars on East 79th Street were jammed bumper to bumper.

Considering the scorn I had felt at the Rosh Hashanah service just two years before, I would have expected myself to be loath to enroll in a class about a religion that seemingly shut me out. It wasn't until my recent committee work for the National Council of Jewish Women that I realized I wanted a better understanding of Judaism.

Bernice had recruited me to volunteer for NCJW, a philanthropic organization she had been a leader in for decades. Although I initially joined the Young Professionals branch out of respect for my mother-in-law, I soon found myself genuinely looking forward to the weekly meetings. The experience of brainstorming with ten vibrant women to create our first fundraising event to benefit a children's literacy program was gratifying except for one nagging concern — I wasn't Jewish. Finally, after months of meetings, I exposed my reservations to my fellow members.

"I'm considering leaving the committee." Sitting cross-legged at a low table in an Upper West Side Japanese restaurant, I felt a wave of relief from my confession.

"What? Why? What's going on?" Judith asked.

Before I could respond, Bonnie jumped in. "It's because you're not Jewish, isn't it?'

"Honestly?" I looked around the table. "Yes. It's the National Council of *Jewish* Women. You're all *Jewish*. I'm not." I fiddled with the napkin on my lap. "Ultimately, I don't belong here."

"Do we make you feel that way?" Judith pressed.

I considered her question for a minute. "No, it's my own feeling. You all seem to have this language, this way of speaking with one another that I can't really be a part of. It's not only here. It's around any group of Jewish people." I bit the inside of my lip. "I don't feel like I'll ever really belong in the Jewish world."

"What do you mean, 'belong'?" Judith asked. With no defensiveness detectable in her voice, she sounded like a partner, helping me explore the nuances of my issues. It felt safe to delve further.

"I don't know," I answered. "It's like, no matter how much I'm around Jews, I feel like there's so much I don't know. Last week Bonnie mentioned a mitzvah and I had no idea what she was talking about. You described your boyfriend as a *mensch* — I didn't understand that, either. And that's just vocabulary…it doesn't even get into the religion of Judaism!"

From my years with Michael I had learned a lot about the Jewish culture and customs. I had researched Jewish traditions when planning our wedding, incorporating them into our civil ceremony. After successive Seders at my mother-in-law's home, I became more and more familiar with the text of the Haggadah, helping me to leave anxiety about pronunciation behind. Pastrami had become my favorite deli food, and I even found myself ordering it on rye bread sans mayo — unthinkable for a Milwaukee girl.

Yet, for all the customs that were becoming part of my life, I still longed for some meaning behind the traditions. I wanted to know what the Sabbath was really about and all the ways the Torah was different from the Bible. But when I asked my friends and Michael's family, they weren't able to answer any of my questions. I was discovering that many Jewish people felt tied to their religion with very little spiritual energy behind their attachment. There had to be more to the Jewish culture than I knew, something so innate that it glued people to it without their being able to verbalize why.

"You know what might help? Taking a class." Judith's suggestion hardly enticed me. After my public snubbing at synagogue, I had no desire to commit to week after week of class, exploring a religion I had no intention of embracing.

"A course? Like what — how to be Jewish? I'm not Jewish. I'm never going to be Jewish." I surprised myself with my rise in emotion.

"No," Judith answered evenly. "A class explaining what being Jewish means."

I thought about Michael's friends and family, the bond they shared from a history they valued. My children would one day be immersed in their world, born into their heritage and being raised Jewish. It made sense that I at least have a basic understanding of the religion.

"Well," I conceded, "I guess it could help."

"I know just the class."

Over tempura and sashimi, Judith described Judaism 101, a course she had recently taken at the 92nd Street Y. I was suspicious. Judith, after all, lit the Sabbath candles every Friday night, never mixed meat with dairy and had been to Israel many times. She would never consider dating anyone who wasn't Jewish. She talked frequently of her mother's leadership role in the Jewish community and was clearly on a similar path. All in all, Judith was what I considered an observant Jew, and it intimidated me. If Judith found Judaism 101 interesting, it would seem graduate-level by my standards.

"What were *you* doing taking that class?" I asked.

"I like the rabbi. He's fantastic. You'll love him. I'll get you the information," she said definitively, as if the matter were closed.

I felt a tiny ripple of excitement. While Judith's knowledge of Judaism was daunting, I envied her understanding of the history of her religion and the spirituality attached to her traditions. I was attracted to the added dimension Judith had to her life, a sense of meaning that cultural Jews didn't possess. Now the same sort of enlightenment could be available to me. My trepidations about the committee evaporated, replaced by a sense of hope.

If I were to take a class in Judaism, however, it was important that Michael enroll with me. After all, although Michael had urged that our children be raised Jewish, for every question I asked about his religion, he simply answered, "What do I know? I'm Jewish. That's all I know." So that very night I pitched my proposal to him.

"How was dinner?" he asked, feet propped up on the coffee table across from the sofa.

"It was great. Judith really helped me."

"With what?"

"Well, you know I've had a lot of questions about Judaism."

"That's great." Michael flipped through the cable channels on the remote. "Judith knows a lot."

"And she suggested I take a class on Judaism at the Y."

Michael pressed another button. "Sounds good."

"And I'd like you to take the class with me."

"Huh?"

"With me. I'd like us to take the class together."

He waved the remote in my direction. "Well, I don't need to take it. I'm already Jewish."

I had predicted this answer and was ready. "Yes, and I'm not. And it would seem, since you insist our children be raised Jewish, that you could learn a little about it yourself." I paused. "That is, unless, you don't want to raise the kids Jewish. Then we can forget the whole thing."

***

I couldn't help but smile as we rushed through the door of the Y before class started, remembering what it was like the first time I had crossed that threshold a few months earlier. Michael had taken me to a concert featuring singers like Bernadette Peters performing numbers from their favorite Broadway productions. Bernice, a subscriber to the highly coveted Lyrics and Lyricists series, was unable to attend the evening's show and generously passed her seats on to us.

When Michael had first told me we were going to the Y on 92nd Street, I was surprised. I hadn't noticed a YMCA on the Upper East Side, only a dilapidated YMCA on our side of the park. I thought back to the YMCA in Milwaukee, with its basketball court, its carpeted floors worn with traffic patterns and weather stains and its modest exercise equipment; I couldn't imagine such a humble institution hosting famous headliners like Broadway singers.

When Michael took my arm amidst a crowd of fashionably dressed people, I marveled that such a glamorous YMCA existed. I stepped onto the marble floor of the vast foyer, looked up at the graceful winding staircase and felt in awe of the elegant, refined architecture. I was equally impressed with the Kaufman Concert Hall, the floor-to-ceiling walnut paneling and crystal chandeliers emanating warmth and elegance. Names of famous artists, etched in gold, floated on the paneling near the ceiling. Sitting in this concert hall, one of a thousand theatergoers, I inhaled the reverence for the arts that surrounded me.

"I have *never* seen a Y like this!" I had exclaimed.

"You've been to a Y before?"

"Sure. The YMCA in Milwaukee."

Michael grinned. "Sally, this is the YMHA."

"YMHA?"

"The Young Men's Hebrew Association."

I leaned my head back in a slow nod, the realization coming over me slowly. *Of course*, I thought. The ambience of the YMHA reflected a starkly different attitude from the religion of my upbringing. The Christians I knew would never have splurged on such a show of extravagance, except in the sanctified setting of a church. With the church as a role model, I had learned to live modestly and with humility, knowing that even if I should come into wealth, I would never live lavishly. Judaism, by evidence of this decor, embraced the beauty of life's riches, believed in the importance of supporting the arts and held in high esteem its impact on our lives.

Now, this winter night, Michael and I walked past the Kaufman Concert Hall and followed the signs to our classroom, climbing the very stairs that had so impressed me. I entered our classroom on the third floor holding Michael's hand, thrilled my husband and I were starting a journey of spiritual learning together. We had taken two classes together — a fiction writing class when we were dating and a ballroom dancing class when we were engaged. Both classes brought us closer together. Now, embarking on religious studies together, I couldn't help but fantasize opening our books at home, preparing for class each week, and discussing what we learned afterward. Our Judaism 101 class could deepen our level of intimacy and commitment to each other.

Entering the classroom, I recalled the contentment I felt as a child walking down our street to mass every Sunday, the priest greeting each of us six kids by name. My mother and father often stood on the pulpit, chosen to read to the congregation from the Bible. Our church friends were an integral part of my preadolescent childhood, camping together, socializing on weekends and holidays.

Now I had agreed to raise our children as Jews, and together Michael and I were about to find out what that meant. I envisioned sharing a religion and feeling at home in a synagogue, just as my parents shared a religion and felt at home in the church. Another piece of my vision of what it meant to be a couple was sliding into place.

The tables, each seating two, were arranged in a semicircle in the cinderblock room. This would be a class full of discussion, a prospect I wasn't completely comfortable with. While I could be counted on as a leader in class participation all through high school and college, I felt very much out of my element here. I would have preferred anonymity. What could I offer this class when I knew nothing about Judaism? I was certain I didn't even have the right terminology to ask questions coherently.

Michael and I pulled out two plastic chairs from a far table and sat down. I assessed my classmates as they straggled in. There were a few 20-something couples and I wondered if they, too, were interfaith, exploring the nuances of the religion they would share. There were half a dozen middle-aged women and men, each apparently taking the class individually. Finally, a handful of senior citizens rounded out the class. Some classmates were dressed in jackets and skirts, most likely having come right from work, while others looked like they lived a life of leisure in jeans and sneakers. Some lay notebooks on their tabletops, others leaned forward, hands clasped between their knees, heels tapping on the floor with nervous energy. All looked around somewhat apprehensively.

I glanced at the clock. It was 7:06. We should have begun our Jewish learning six minutes ago. I smiled anxiously at Michael and pretended to be comfortable, fighting against my instinct to grab my spiral-bound notebook and bolt, sure that "non-Jew ignoramus" was written all over my face. It would be easy enough — we could pretend we realized we were in the wrong classroom and slip out the door. Certain that Michael would happily reclaim his Tuesday nights, I knew it would be easy to persuade him. If I felt this uneasy in Judaism 101, surely everyone around me knew I didn't belong here.

I remembered what my father told me during a visit to Milwaukee. Sitting at a local diner for a rare breakfast alone together, he asked how serious I was with Michael.

"Pretty serious."

"You know, they have a name for you."

"They? Who's 'they'?"

"Jewish people."

I sighed, knowing where he was going. "I know, dad. It's slang, and it's never—"

"*Shiksa*. Any woman who is not Jewish is a shiksa according to the Jews." My father nodded knowingly. "They actually have a label for anyone who is not one of them." He set his coffee down and picked up a laminated menu. "Just so you know."

I had dismissed my father's concerns. Michael had never referred to me by such a term, not even jokingly, nor had any other Jewish person I knew. In fact, because the only time I heard the word was when Michael's great-aunt Molly said her friend's son was "dating a shiksa," I assumed it was a word from her generation.

I already felt white-bread Midwestern, recalling how I revealed myself as an outsider for not knowing there was a Jewish Y. If I didn't know something as fundamental as that, learning about the Jewish religion now seemed as vast and unbearable as a trek across a desert. I suddenly felt that I was, indeed, very much a shiksa.

To make matters worse, there was a lot I didn't know about Catholicism either. For someone who attended church every Sunday through adolescence, I could only name a few books from the Old and New Testaments, and of those, I could only loosely state the subject matter of Genesis. I felt like a fraud in every direction — a Catholic who really wasn't Catholic, a non-Jew attending a class about Judaism.

The rabbi burst into the classroom. Striding through the open door, he dropped his notebook and books onto the bare tabletop at the front of the room and grabbed the dry-erase marker from the tray. He scrawled his name and *Judaism 101*across the board.

I had very few preconceived notions about rabbis, except for the image of the elderly, bearded wise men in yarmulkes gracing the big screen in *Fiddler on the Roof* and *Yentl*. Growing up in the Southside of Milwaukee, I never had occasion to meet any clergy of the Jewish faith.

This rabbi's exuberance was contagious. When he turned and smiled at the class, my notions of a tense, awkward environment were replaced with visions of a lively, upbeat class.

Reading his slanted scrawl on the board, I recalled some key phrases from the class description — *If you never learned much about Judaism but suspect there may be something to it* and *Learn the basics of Judaism in a welcoming and relaxed atmosphere* — and calmed myself. Of course, this was exactly the class that would enlighten me.

"Okay! We're in Judaism 101. Everyone in the right place?" The rabbi ran his thick fingers through his bushy brown hair and looked around the classroom, pacing back and forth in front of the dry-erase board.

We all glanced side to side.

"Okay, then. Let's start by introducing ourselves." He threw his arm out in front of him. "Let's start here. Tell us who you are and why you're here."

And so the dreaded roundtable began. The method of getting to know one another through awkward monologues never served me well. Typically I counted ahead to see how many people were before me. As I got to the under-five count, I tuned out, rehearsing my own introduction. When I realized that my minimal speech was bound to be insignificant and that everyone would be staring at me, my heart raced. I would reflect how unusual that was considering my resting heart rate is reliably 60 beats per minute, a fact of which I am particularly proud. I would then try to determine if my heart rate had hit 120. At my turn, I would blurt out whatever came to mind, and within a minute after my fumbling introduction, my heart rate would go back to its healthy resting rate.

The introductions in Judaism 101 were starkly different. I listened intently, leaning forward against the Formica table, wanting very much to hear each person's motivations for signing up for this ten-week course. Specifically, I was listening for someone to reveal that they were not Jewish.

The first woman described a desire to find out why her parents ignored their Jewish faith, teaching her nothing about Judaism at all. The next student described his desire to delve deeper into the meaning of his family's traditions. The third told of her grandfather passing away. After sitting shiva, she realized she knew very little about her heritage. And so it went around the room, classmates describing their search for meaning in a religion that was already theirs. As I heard each tale, I felt like a cardboard figure slowly being pulled into the background of a diorama. My heart pounded against my chest as my turn approached, and I envisioned getting up and saying, "Oh! Judaism 101? I was looking for a sewing class!" and scooting out behind my seated classmates, Michael, mystified, following after me. Right before the rabbi rested his eyes on me, a voice screeched inside my head, *Why did you sit to Michael's right? Now you have to be the one to go first! You don't belong here! You're not Jewish!!*

"Hi." I meekly smiled. "My name is Sally Friedes. This is my husband, Michael. He's Jewish and I'm not. And I, uh, wanted to learn about the Jewish religion."

Weak! I verbally slapped myself. *That doesn't begin to tell why you're here!*

"Okay." The rabbi smiled. He looked to Michael.

"And I'm the husband."

"Uh huh. Great. And were you raised observant?"

"No," he chuckled uncomfortably. "Not at all."

There were just two classmates left to introduce themselves. They, too, were Jewish.

When the introductions were finished, the rabbi told us about the format of the class. "We're going to discuss all of the basics of Judaism. The Ten Commandments. Rituals. Rites of passage. Traditions. And you'll learn the meanings of all of these in your Jewish life. Let's start with rituals. Who can tell me about a ritual in Judaism?"

I leaned back in my plastic chair and smiled to myself. Nothing exploded when I confessed that I wasn't Jewish. The rabbi didn't single me out. I had simply been hypersensitive. I had conquered my inner demons, swept away that devil on my shoulder as easily as flicking away a fly. I had finally opened the door to my Jewish education. I tuned back into the rabbi.

"...and there are many rituals around a Jewish marriage. But first let me be clear. I do not believe in interfaith marriage."

I was startled. Could I have heard him correctly? Could the rabbi really be saying what I thought he said?

"I do not think it is good for the Jews. I do not think it is good for families. And I will not perform an interfaith ceremony. Not under any circumstances."

I sat, motionless, fixing my eyes on the rabbi. I did not want to witness the 20 pairs of eyes that were surely boring into me. In them I would read their pity, superiority, judgment, even embarrassment on my behalf. I couldn't even look at Michael and only wished he would reach to touch my hand under the table. It felt as if all other tables were drawn away from me, and I sat in the middle of the room, isolated and alone in the middle of the linoleum floor.

"So let's move on to the Ten Commandments," the rabbi continued.

My heels pressed into the floor. No rabbi was going to exclude me from this conversation, not even this intimidating figure before me. For years I had felt like an outsider at Passover and Jewish gatherings and I was tired of it. In the face of the rabbi's disdain, I was suddenly convicted in my determination to break the code, uncovering what made Jews so unshakably attached to their heritage. Reaching for the unattainable was nothing new for me. I had earned a scholarship to study fashion in London, beating hundreds of applicants even though I technically did not qualify for the program. As a college student, I landed an internship at a prestigious retailer in Chicago and was flown via Lear jet across the country to visit manufacturing plants. Days after graduating college, I moved to Manhattan sans job or apartment — knowing virtually no one —having never been to New York City before. I was offered the job of my choice on the first interview. I had faced mountains and scaled them . I was not going to walk out of this class. Instead I leaned forward, determined to squeeze out every bit of information I paid for in my class tuition.

"Who can tell me the First Commandment?"

"Uh, isn't it something about God being the only God?" a middle-aged man meekly volunteered.

"Yes — 'Thou shall have no other gods before Me.' What does this mean?"

Classmates adjusted themselves in their seats and glanced at one another. I suddenly realized that I wasn't the only one uncomfortable in this class. Jew or non-Jew, many of us felt we were coming into the class lacking important knowledge. Only it was worse for the Jews — they felt inferior in the knowledge they thought they should have. Not being Jewish, I had nothing to lose in exposing my ignorance. I shot my hand up in the air, forcing the rabbi to include the class shiksa.

"It is forbidden to worship pagan gods."

"That's correct." The rabbi glanced in my direction and pointed around the class. "But how can it be interpreted by today's standards?"

It had never occurred to me to interpret the commandments in contemporary context. Throughout my childhood, I had struggled to place myself in biblical times, trying to understand the commandments in historical conditions. What had it been like to worship pagan gods? Did people really dance around statues? How could that possibly be relevant today?

"What might we worship today?" the rabbi urged. "What are we tempted to make our god?"

"Money!" "Power!" "Status!" "Beauty!"

And it clicked. One commandment after another was interpreted by modern standards, and guidelines for living were slowly being constructed. "Thou shall not murder" meant not only the literal killing of one human being by another; it also prohibited extinguishing the spirit of others. How often had my spirit been dampened by the criticism of a teacher or the indifference of a friend? "Thou shall not covet thy neighbor's house and wife" could be expanded beyond the envy of possessions to include the desire for someone else's life and lifestyle. As a Midwestern girl who was raised by parents of modest means, it was a fresh reminder to avoid looking enviously at the abundance of others in Manhattan.

I liked what I was hearing but I was still stinging, unable to get past the assault of the rabbi's comment. Walking out with Michael after class, I asked him what he had thought.

"What did *you* think?"

"It's a mix. I can't believe he said that in the beginning of class."

"I know. Me, too. Don't take it personally."

"It is personal. I'm personally not Jewish."

Michael never attended another class. I'd like to say he did so in protest of the rabbi's statement, but it had more to do with his disinterest. He was Jewish. What was there to question?

Stuck in my stubbornness, I did go to the next class, but left by the 90-minute break. No matter how enticing the subject matter, how enlightening the discussion, I wouldn't be able to participate in Judaism 101 with the level of enthusiasm innate to me. I had walked into the first class, my mix of trepidation and excitement a neon target for the rabbi's insensitive remark. My spirit had been murdered. I took away the most basic concept of Judaism of all — to be included in a conversation about Judaism, one needed to actually be Jewish.

Strawberry Yogurt Shake

I loved being around Jewish people. Their energy and forthrightness was a magnet to me, their candor a welcome addition to my life. While I grew up in a family that enjoyed big gatherings, their exchanges paled in comparison to the intellectual sparring and candid conversations with Michael's circle. With friends bluntly telling one another when they were being rude and cousins ceaselessly teasing each other about their quirks, I reveled in the environment of nothing left unsaid.

I became an enthusiastic participant in Jewish rituals, too, breaking matzah with Michael's family at Passover and constructing menorahs at Hanukkah parties. When the first few bars of "Hava Nagila" played at Jewish weddings, I was the first one out of my seat clasping the hands of strangers and dancing in a circle around the bride and groom hoisted up in chairs.

But it wasn't until my pregnancy with Harrison that I became immersed in the Jewish way of life. It started one day in a crowded Upper West Side baby-supply store.

"We'd like the crib delivered the day the baby is born," Michael instructed the grandmotherly saleswoman.

I leaned back in a glider, waiting for my husband to complete the order, my stomach bursting with seven months of growing fetus. The dozens of mobiles were dizzying, the pastel farm animals and black-and-white psychedelic spirals hovering and twirling over the sea of browsing couples. The dazed expressions of the other customers reflected my feelings of utter and complete mystification. Why was there such a vast assortment of rattles, teething rings, changing tables, cribs, toddler beds and other baby paraphernalia? How was I to decide which diaper was the most absorbent or which pacifier the most soothing?

Surveying my surroundings, I calculated that there had to be more than a hundred items per square foot. Who could possibly process all of this information? Within minutes of entering the crowded store, the low ceilings seemed to be descending on me. My head felt dizzy and my blood sugar dropped, a Pavlovian response to too much stimulation. An hour later, having selected a crib following an exasperating debate, I was anxious to get home to our quiet, uncluttered apartment. I was tired of being bumped around by other pregnant bellies and wanted to enjoy the one gratifying experience of the day — knowing that our baby's crib was on its way.

Now, hearing Michael's instruction to delay the delivery, my irritation escalated. "Wait until the baby is born?" I measured my words. "How are we supposed to know when that is?"

Michael turned to the saleswoman, who was already nodding conspiratorially.

"No problem, darling." The chain on her glasses swayed. "You'll call us from the hospital and we'll deliver everything."

"What? Call from the hospital? Let's just have it delivered this weekend. We can get everything set up."

The vision of a completed nursery had thrilled me. Since childhood, I'd nurtured images of being a mother, starting with the preparation of the nursery. It was a romantic notion, the thought of my husband and me beginning our journey as parents, everything ahead of us new and unpredictable. I pictured assembling the crib and painting the baby's room together, giddy with anticipation.

I knew now this was not to be.

"Why can't we have the crib this weekend?"

"Oh, no...we don't do that." Michael shook his head.

"Don't do what?"

"We don't have the crib delivered. We don't have anything delivered."

"We don't? Why not?" I asked, wondering who 'we' was.

"Because it's bad luck. "

"Bad luck? What do you mean, 'bad luck'?" I could feel my hormones churning.

"Well...you know."

Suddenly I understood. He was referring to some sort of Jewish superstition, something I had never heard of before.

"Like something-will-happen-to-the-baby bad luck?"

"Well, no. It's more that, uh, if something happens to the baby, it's just, you know, too painful to take apart the nursery."

Always one for a sharp retort or a sarcastic response, I was unexpectedly without words. It was unthinkable that something might happen to my baby. In fact, just considering it seemed to curse the pregnancy.

"Okay," I said, meekly. "We'll wait."

My stomach clenched. Now, not only was I forced to worry about getting an entire nursery assembled after giving birth, but Michael's words were destined to haunt me.

It had never occurred to me that something could go wrong with my pregnancy. Four of my siblings had had babies already and no one had experienced any complications whatsoever. I had been enjoying my pregnancy bliss, watching my stomach expand, feeling the baby kick. But now, with Michael's words, I recalled the baby of my mom's hairdresser, born with severe disabilities. I remembered an acquaintance's stillbirth. I suddenly imagined myself standing in an empty, beautifully furnished nursery— without a child.

I later found out there was more to the Jewish tradition of delaying setting up the nursery. Some Jews believed that by holding off on decorating a nursery, they would not attract evil spirits. This only extended the notion of silly superstition to me and seemed more lore than wisdom. However, when a friend told me that Jews believe pregnancy is a precious time, a time to be reveled in, a period for a quiet state of happiness and prayerful optimism, the gloomy feeling around the tradition of delaying the nursery was lifted, replaced with a lightness of peace, patience and validation.

Time and again I told my friends how much I loved being pregnant, feeling at one with the child growing, kicking, and turning, inside my body. I had no desire to plan for the nursery. I wanted only to delight in my pregnancy. It seemed Jewish tradition enacted what I couldn't explain. I couldn't envision life with a baby I hadn't yet met. I could only delight in the miracle of my pregnant state.

But, as I sat in the glider with the sun waning outside the store window, I hadn't known the various pieces of Jewish wisdom that were the cause of my disappointment. I only knew how hard it would be to pull the baby's room together, particularly as the wife of an interior designer. As particular as Michael always was about his home, it only escalated after he launched his own interior decorating company. He taped 2-inch-square paint chips to our walls for weeks before deciding on a color, often only to reverse his decision after one wall had been painted and starting the entire process over. Fabric swatches appeared by the dozens, splayed across chairs, and it wasn't unusual to find Michael rearranging furniture and artwork late into the night. The nursery was no different. Not only was it not painted, we didn't have diapers, clothing or baby bottles. Now, to top it off, we wouldn't even have the crib delivered.

***

In the next few months we continued designing the nursery — hypothetically. Ordering the cream-colored crib with distressed blue trim had been checked off our list, and Michael spent weeks shopping and selecting fabrics for the glider cushion, bedding, window treatments and even diaper pad. The manila folder of final decisions thickened with fabric swatches, magazine tear sheets, business cards, carpet samples and floor plans. It was a virtual room — none of these items actually entered our apartment. I resigned myself to the notion that if I wanted to see the baby's room, all I needed to do was open the file and browse.

My mother-in-law's involvement in my pregnancy was another shock. While my own mother rarely asked how I was feeling or how an obstetrician's appointment had gone, Bernice was a veritable watchdog of my health. I was, after all, the incubator, the keeper of her most precious gem: her unborn first grandchild.

"Sally, are you eating enough? You're looking too thin. Michael, get her another serving of chicken, will you please?"

"Did you register for a layette? I'm going to buy one for you. Can you meet me at Bloomie's on Friday?"

"Dear, I read in the *Times* today that folic acid is very important for the baby's brain development. Did you see that article? I've saved it for you."

Bernice even monitored my safety. "Sally! Don't go outside today!" She called me on wintry mornings. "It's treacherous! You could slip and fall. You should work out of the apartment today."

Having recently left my fashion career to become partner in Friedes Associates Interior Design, a company launched by Michael, it was possible I could have worked from home, but I never acquiesced. The last thing I wanted was an invisible tether across Central Park from my mother-in-law's apartment to my expanded belly. Yet, just as I had adjusted to a nursery-in-concept-only, I slowly surrendered to Bernice's participation, adjusting to her fixation on my pregnancy. On some level I even liked it — having a container of my favorite strawberry yogurt handed to me every time I sat at Bernice's table and receiving her many caring calls from across town. For the first time in my life,

I felt truly cosseted.

***

While receiving the adoring attention of a Jewish mother, I inadvertently found myself becoming a thoughtful Jewish daughter. During one of my mother's visits from Colorado, I took her and Bernice to witness an ultrasound at my obstetrician's office. It seemed a perfect time to share my pregnancy with my mother, from whom I still fantasized an enthusiastic reaction. I also knew Bernice would treasure a preview of her grandchild.

Minutes after entering the Park Avenue medical office, I was propped at a 30-degree angle on the examining table, my maternity top rolled above my stomach, the nurse dragging a wand over my girth. I instructed my mother and mother-in-law to watch the monitor to my right.

"Joyce! Look!" Bernice exclaimed.

"Oh, my gosh! Would you look at that! The baby is sucking his thumb! I can't believe it. He's sucking his thumb!!"

"He is! He's sucking his thumb!" Bernice joined in. "Hold on. Can you tell it's a boy?" She walked around my elevated feet and leaned into the monitor.

"Well, no...I'm just saying that, you know, the baby...!"

"Don't tell me!" I called out from above my stomach, the cold jelly oozing to my former waistline. "I don't want to know the gender!"

"Isn't this amazing..." my mother marveled, her cheeks flushing.

"I've never seen anything like it," Bernice agreed. "We didn't have sonograms when we were pregnant, did we, Joyce?"

"Well, I should say not!" My mother laughed. "Can you imagine what would have happened if I had seen the twins like this? I might not have gone home and had so much wine!"

As the grandmothers stood over my exposed belly, comparing

notes on their own pregnancies, a feeling of contentment washed over me. Bernice was in her element, completely involved in my pregnancy, and my mother was unabashed in her positive fervor. There we were, three women, watching my baby — their grandchild — move in my stomach, just inches from where they stood.

Afterward, under the skylight of an Upper East Side pub, we brainstormed about the baby's name. I told my mother what Michael had explained to me: in the Jewish tradition, babies are named after a loved one who has passed away, typically using that person's first initial. Michael and I had agreed to name our baby after his late father, Harry. I thought it a touching way to pay tribute to a man I had never known, but whom Michael and his family dearly missed. We confirmed the baby's first initial would be *H* and went through a process struggling for a name we could agree on. I had pushed for Hubbell, a main character in the movie *The Way We Were*, but Michael scoffed. I loved Hope, but Michael considered it too obvious a reflection of my zealous outlook on life. He went on an Irish bent, jotting a list that included Griffin, Duncan and Ian, hoping to transplant the *H* to the middle name, but I dismissed each of them. We were finally able to narrow down our choices to Harrison or Hannah, but couldn't commit to them until we had a middle-name combination that pleased us. We were stumped.

Amazingly, before we were even served our charbroiled burgers, Bernice and Joyce effortlessly arrived at two perfect name options for our baby: Hannah Rose or Harrison Scott. The choices rang in perfection and at that moment, I hadn't a worry or concern about anything. I delighted in the attention of Bernice and my mother. My mother-in-law illuminated the nurturing side of Joyce, and in turn, my mother drew out Bernice's stories of mothering infants, memories that seemed to surprise Bernice herself. A spirit of motherhood unified all three of us.

Hours later, as I hugged Bernice goodbye outside a waiting cab, it occurred to me that I had involved my mother-in-law in my pregnancy long before conception.

"Michael isn't ready to have a baby," I blurted over dinner with Bernice once day. "And I am! I don't know what to do!"

The year before, Michael and I had agreed to start a family. We enjoyed the sanctity of our secret, looking forward to the day we would go public with the announcement of my pregnancy. But just one month after I suspended my birth-control prescription, he had changed his mind, declaring he wasn't ready. "Let's wait awhile — you know — till the business takes off," he had said. I knew Bernice was my best chance of changing my husband's mind.

"What does he mean, he's 'not ready'? What is he waiting for?"

"He's worried about finances and how our lifestyle will change. He feels very stressed about it."

"But doesn't he see?" Bernice screeched. "His waiting won't change that! He'll have the same objections two years from now." She paused, startled by the truth of her words. "Or more!"

"I know! And the thing is, he was ready last year. But he's changed his mind."

"What do you mean, 'changed his mind'? Why would he do that?"

I recounted how my oldest brother, Steve, inadvertently foiled our original plan for pregnancy. A father of two, he and his wife, Chris, were staying with us for a spontaneous visit without the kids. Sitting on a knoll in Central Park overlooking the Great Lawn, Steve ruminated about his life.

"Kids...," he grumbled. "Man, oh man, they change your life forever."

"What do you mean? Michael looked over at him, startled. "You're glad you have kids, aren't you?"

Chris smiled and shushed Steve, chuckling and imploring him to say that it wasn't that bad. But I knew it was too late. The damage had been done. Later that week, at Michael's insistence, I called in a new prescription for the pill. Since that day, I had urged and begged and rationalized my desire to start a family, but nothing had worked.

I gazed down at the tablecloth. "It's been a year. I'm just out of options."

"Oh, no, you're not. I've got it!" The stemware rattled with the slap of her palms on the table. "You tell him that from now on the burden of birth control is on him. If he doesn't want to have a baby, then it's up to him to make sure it doesn't happen." She hit the table again like a judge slamming a gavel on the podium. "That'll take care of it."

"His responsibility..." I turned the thought over and over in my head. "It makes perfect sense..."

"Of course it does. Why should you have to worry about it?" Bernice lifted her chin at a passing uniform, raising her hand. "Waiter! A glass of wine, please."

Bernice must have known what she was doing, because three months later Michael gave me a beautiful card with a picture of a baby on it. His inscription read, "I really am ready... and I'm so excited!" That night I walked out of the bathroom, dumbfounded, holding a little white stick with a pink stripe. I was pregnant.

***

One morning, in the beginning of my third trimester, I lay in bed unable to move, severe abdominal cramps shooting pain to every limb.

"I'm sure it was just the spicy food I ate," I told Michael, referring to the Indian meal he had made the night before. "There's no reason to call the doctor. I'll be okay."

"Sally," he pleaded. "Look at you. You're in such pain, you can barely breathe."

"Then you should've used less curry."

Calling my obstetrician at 6 am on a Sunday morning seemed self-indulgent. What if there was nothing wrong? I didn't want to intrude on my doctor's time for a false alarm.

"Fine. Then I'll call."

An hour later, admitted to the hospital, hooked up to monitors, I wondered how things had gone so bad so quickly. The complications in my pregnancy were serious. Diagnosed with preeclampsia, at any moment my blood pressure could have skyrocketed, causing seizures. In addition, I was in preterm labor, something that turned out to be a positive twist of fate. Had I not had the cramping, it wasn't likely we would have discovered my preeclampsia — a condition that could have resulted in my baby's death or my own.

Hearing the doctor's order to stay on modified bed rest for the remainder of my pregnancy threw me into a panic. I was in the middle of invoicing clients and calculating quarterly projections. It seemed impossible that I couldn't return to work. I immediately compiled a list of files for Michael to retrieve from the office so I could work from home.

During my five-day stay in the hospital, amidst calls of concern and support from my family in Wisconsin, my New York friends and family visited, almost always with the gift of food. Bernice came by every day with lunch and a Scrabble board, stating that no one could ever beat her but that she'd play if I really wanted to. Aunt Joan called several times, assuring me that the preterm labor was not my fault, that the baby would be fine, and that she would be happy to bring me dinner.

On the first day of my stay, Nicky called to see if she could bring me something.

"A strawberry yogurt shake would be great," I answered, somewhat meekly. An hour later, Nicky entered my hospital room, her voice resounding before I even saw her face.

"Do you have any idea how hard it is to find a freakin' strawberry yogurt drink in my neighborhood?" She plopped a wrinkled white bag on my rolling food tray, as she would every day for the next five days, and smiled. "Here's your damn milkshake."

It struck me how far I had come in my relationships with Michael's friends. Years ago I could barely get through a dinner with Michael's closest friends, feeling alienated by their inside jokes and banter. Now I was an integral part of their world. Nicky's teasing proved it.

It also didn't take long for me to realize that in the Jewish world, caring for someone meant more than calling or showing up — it meant bringing food. It was a type of nurturing I hadn't experienced before. In my family, a sore throat might receive a delicious concoction of blended raw egg, milk and nutmeg, but even that didn't happen often. With six children, a sick person lying on the sofa was a common sight. No one whispered around the limp, feverish patient. If the sickly wanted quiet, they needed to go to another room.

In the Jewish culture, food was a show of generosity, a gift that made me feel nurtured and valued. Food was not only part of a gathering or celebration — it was an expression. At Beth's wedding, the sumptuous dinner felt like a show of gratitude to her guests. The bagels, lox and spreads at baby namings were a display of tradition, reminding us that our gathering was specifically Jewish. Even casually visiting a friend's house, food was always offered immediately. Now, in the hospital, every delivery of a meal or snack to my bedside felt like an offering of sustenance, and I was deeply moved. So much about the offering of food was not about the food itself. It was a declaration that someone was looking out for me, foreseeing my needs before I even thought about them. When a friend called on the way to the hospital offering to bring lunch, I'd look at my watch, not having realized it was time for me to eat — but she had thought of it for me. When I arrived at someone's home and there was food awaiting me, it felt like an open-arms welcome into the home. The kitchen is the heart of the home, and with food as an extension of the kitchen, I was being welcomed into their hearts.

More than anything, it was the joy in which food was shared that struck me. In the gatherings of my childhood, I got the sense that the summer sausage and other hors d'oeuvres were on the table because they *should* be — it was what one did when entertaining. At Jewish gatherings, the food was presented with a generous spirit. "Sally. Did you eat? Please, have more." Often food was scooped onto my plate at the dinner table, and always in generous portions. With the food, there was unconditional love.

Food was just an element in a broader code of conduct in Michael's brand of Jewishness. In his circle, when people had celebrations, tribulations or sufferings, boundaries were toppled and replaced with openhanded generosity. It was a code of ethics I unconsciously adopted as I became entrenched in my husband's world. Whenever I received an invitation to a fundraiser, I read the list of committee members and responded with either a positive RSVP or a donation. When a friend was in the hospital, I visited, always calling first to see what I could bring. When my sister Chrissy told me a close friend had been diagnosed with cancer, I suggested she prepare meals for the family immediately, and often, without being asked.

Yet at no other time did I feel I'd been initiated into the Jewish community more than when Harrison was born. Minutes after giving birth, lying on a gurney in a corridor of the overcrowded hospital, holding my swaddled son, I heard the irritated voice of a nurse down the hall.

"No, I'm sorry, ma'am. You cannot go down there. This area is for patients only."

"But please, I'm the grandmother!"

I turned to Michael. "Is that your mother?" I asked incredulously. I had only gone into labor less than two hours before and already my mother-in-law was at the hospital.

"Uh, yes."

"When on earth did you call your mother? Couldn't you have waited until after the baby was born?"

"Well, I was excited!"

I held tight to the cloud of intimacy still fogging us in from the outside world.

"Please. My son called me. My grandson is down there. Really, I'll be only a second."

And just like that, the cloud dissipated and Bernice appeared, her arms outstretched. I had been holding my newborn son for less than an hour; I wasn't ready to let go of him.

Tears puddled in Bernice's eyes as she lifted her gaze from my swaddled baby and onto me. "How are you, dear?"

She leaned forward and kissed my cheek. She was reaching for me, not Harrison.

I smiled. "I'm great."

Bernice looked at the bundle on my chest and pulled back the blanket.

"Oh, my goodness!"

"Would you like to hold him?"

She gingerly cradled her first grandchild in her arms. "Michael! He looks just like me!" she blurted.

***

The next day our hospital room was host to a revolving stream of friends and family. Arriving with stuffed animals and balloons, their faces beaming, they congratulated us on our newborn son. Even parents of our friends called and sent gifts. Perched on my hospital bed, fully recovered from my short delivery, I joyously offered my bundled baby to anyone comfortable enough to hold him. Harrison was the first baby among our friends, and I loved passing him around to each person, knowing the only way I could express the joy I was feeling was to have them experience it themselves. Norman and Joan, Nicky and Debbie…every person who entered the room welcomed our son into their world.

I didn't know it then, but I later learned that this sense of community is the essence of Judaism. Torah study can only occur with a *minyan* — a group of ten adults — because the spirit of the text can only come to life when it is expressed between people. In fact, most Jewish prayers are written in the plural, "us" instead of "me," emphasizing our responsibility and connectedness to one another. Life-cycle events such as weddings and births are not to be private affairs either, but are to be celebrated with the community, allowing friends and family to revel in the joy of the event, thereby multiplying the blessing of the occasion.

Watching people rock baby Harrison in their arms, their eyes connecting with my son's, I saw he was embraced by a roomful of friends and family who were brimming with joy. Harrison was not only the child of Michael and me. He was joining a large community of loving, generous, thoughtful people, a group who loved him unconditionally.

Dinner in the Hamptons

"This may be the last good corn of the season," Bernice said, taking her seat next to her boyfriend, Harold.

It was my favorite time of day in the Hamptons. The birds chirped their evening songs from the thick woods outside Bernice's house, the rays of the sinking sun reaching like fingers between the branches of the tall pines. I kept Harrison on my lap for a moment at the dinner table, enjoying the warmth of his legs on mine before slipping him into his high chair.

"I know... and then before we know it, it's time for the High Holy Days." Amy, Michael's niece, scooted her chair closer to the table. I always considered Amy's company refreshing. Just a few years younger than me, she was leading the life of a roving artist.

"When is Rosh Hashanah this year?" Michael asked.

I was happy to disassociate myself from this conversation. I was already on edge from two days in the country. Aside from the company of the family, I didn't relish being in the Hamptons. The throngs of New Yorkers who descended on the idyllic seaside villages every weekend were intrusive, their horn honking and loud cell-phone conversations more suitable to Wall Street than the serene setting of the beach towns. So crowded were the weekends that the stunning stretch of white sand beaches dotted with shingled mansions and rolling dunes were often inaccessible due to overcrowded parking lots.

"Are the High Holy Days in September?" Michael turned to his mother.

"The beginning of October."

Years had passed since my first — and only — temple experience at Rosh Hashanah — a miserable two hours I wanted to forget. Since then, any conversation remotely about Judaism was my cue to tune out and turn my thoughts elsewhere. This time my mind went to the 20-mile bike ride I had returned from just one hour earlier.

Soaring up and down hills to Three Mile Harbor, along Sag Harbor Bay, through the Northwest Woods and beside the potato fields of Bridgehampton, my late afternoon bike rides immersed me in the region's irresistible charm. At a lonely dead-end road by the bay, fishermen held long poles and nets, wading knee high in the water, skimming for clams. Several miles inland, the wind rippled the wheat fields, stalks swaying in unison. Further down the road horses grazed nose to nose, oblivious to the random sports cars zipping along the winding country lane. Even now, after Harrison's birth, I still managed to make time for the bike rides I relished.

My rides were my commune with nature, a connecting with God. Day to day, my mind was inundated with thoughts of to-do lists, schedules and plans. But when I rode my bike through the countryside, my thoughts were only on the wonders of nature. How beautiful were the different shades of green against the translucent blue sky! The multitude of wildflower colors inter-mingled in perfect balance, the branches of trees whispering in the wind, a hushed symphony of motion. I didn't have a church or congregation to root me in my spirituality, but nature always filled the void.

"That's not for a month," Michael exclaimed, calculating the dates. "It's late this year!"

Like every other Jewish person I knew, Michael attended temple on Rosh Hashanah and Yom Kippur, regardless of whether he stepped foot into a synagogue during the rest of the year. Growing up, I had learned a "good Catholic" attended church every single Sunday. Which is what my family did. Each Sunday morning, we dressed in our Sunday best, devoured our breakfast of pancakes and sausages, and walked half a block down our sidewalk to Our Lady of Lourdes. And being good Catholics gave us unspoken permission to turn and tsk-tsk the families at Christmas Mass who showed up only for major holidays. Not only were they definitely not "good Catholics," they interfered with our seating. My family always located themselves in the third row, near our friends. But during the holiday masses, the parents shot each other commiserating glances from across the back of the church, while the Christmas Catholics, having arrived one hour earlier, sat in our seats, oblivious to our displacement.

When Michael and other Jews went only to the High Holy Day services, I assumed they ranked pretty low in the "good-Jew" category. I wondered how they could be comfortable with that status. How could most Jews I knew be content with going to temple only once a year? Were they using those visits simply as a means to appease their guilt for missing services the rest of the year? Was that all Judaism was about? I knew there had to be more to it, even though the Jews I knew couldn't tell me what that might be. Earlier in the year I had met two rabbis at a cocktail party and I was struck by how lit up they were, talking about their religion. As close as my family was to the priests of our parish, I couldn't recall any of them being as excited about Catholicism as these two rabbis were about Judaism. Even though the rabbi at the 92nd Street Y had discouraged me from continuing my studies, I had to admit that he seemed intoxicated with his love for Judaism.

"Are you joining us this year, dear?" Bernice set down her crystal beer stein. I dipped my burger into a dollop of ketchup waiting for Amy to respond. Then I noticed all eyes on me. I quickly swallowed my bite.

"Huh? Well, I don't know. I mean—"

"Mom, we've got Harrison," Michael jumped in, protecting

both his wife and mother from a potential clash.

"Can't that nice lady Hazel take care of him? She sits for you a few times a week."

Heat swelled in my chest as I remembered my humiliation the last time I had gone to synagogue. The rabbi had declared his disdain for interfaith marriages, confirming in my mind that I was an outcast. I decided to clear the air as diplomatically as possible.

"I just don't know why I'd go to temple again, Bernice."

"Uh, oh...," Michael mumbled

"Why not?" my mother-in-law asked, seemingly surprised.

"The last time I went wasn't exactly enjoyable." I tried hard to restrain myself from telling Bernice that not only did I have no interest in Judaism, I would consider my absence from temple a statement *against* the religion.

"I can understand that," Harold interjected. "My father died when I was five, and my mother made me go to *shul* every day for a year. Every day after school I'd have to sit in shul by myself for one hour," he took a gulp of his beer. "When that year was over, I never went again."

Harold's recollection only cemented my belief that there was little rationale to the principles of Judaism. Imagining a sweet kindergartner, his head barely visible above the back of the pew, alone in a vast sanctuary, I shook my head.

After hearing the rabbi rail against interfaith marriage, I had been compelled to uncover some of the reasons Jews felt such conviction about sticking together. Some of my Jewish girlfriends would only date Jews. Michael's relatives were upset that his cousin was dating a non-Jew. All around me, there was so much devotion to keeping Judaism alive that I couldn't help but think it was a race they were protecting, not a religion. In fact, I was having trouble getting at just what the religion was about.

"What, exactly, do Jews believe?" I had once asked a circle of Michael's friends.

"Well, I don't know," they looked around uncomfortably.

One friend struggled for an answer, "I know what we don't believe — we don't believe in Jesus."

"But, why not?" I prodded.

"I don't know. We just don't."

"How are you different from Christians?"

"Oh, please. We're different."

"What do you believe about life after death? Do you believe in reincarnation? In heaven?"

"I don't know."

"Do you believe in God?"

"Yeah, I guess so."

Conversations like these confirmed that the foundation of Judaism was tradition, not spirituality. I had hoped the rituals would lead me to some degree of insight about myself and my relationship to the world.

I remembered watching the family light the candles in *Fiddler on the Roof*, the room seeming magical with the glowing candles and the singing in minor key. From images like these, I had expected a mystical ambience to Jewish rituals. Time and again I had joined Michael as he lit Hanukkah candles, thinking it would be nice to understand the blessing, or at least to pause in reflection or gratitude. Instead, Michael pushed through the rote blessing and quickly moved on to gift opening. I concluded that the rules and observances in Judaism were in place only to honor heritage.

Although I was disillusioned with the Catholic Church, I still yearned for a religion that deepened my ability to feel God's presence. With the hectic and vibrant pace of New York City confronting me every day, more and more I felt the need to be grounded.

Unable to unearth any satisfying answers about Judaism, I turned to other organized religions. I attended a service at the Universalist Church on Central Park West, where 50 people listened to a minister talk about the importance of charity. While the middle-aged congregants seemed nice enough, extending themselves with introductions and offering information on the church, the idea that each person should be allowed to develop their own personal theology seemed anything but unifying.

I attended a few services at the Science of Mind Church at Lincoln Center, where a thousand people clasped hands across the aisle, singing "Let There Be Peace on Earth." While I enjoyed the self-help books sold in the lobby, many written by the founder of the church, Ernest Holmes, the vast size of the membership and the church's emphasis on the mind, rather than the spirit, did not draw me in.

I had begun to think my quest would not end happily. Either I would never discover a religion that felt fulfilling and my spiritual life would not be nurtured; or I would and then I would be lonely, attending services without Michael and Harrison.

Harrison clanged a stainless steel fork on the table, watching it fall to the floor.

"Listen," I tried to explain, "after the rabbi's sermon last time, I really don't feel the need—"

"What sermon?"

"You don't remember?"

Although Bernice and I had never discussed the rabbi's sermon, I assumed it was because she was embarrassed.

"What did the rabbi say?"

"Basically, that I shouldn't have married Michael."

"He said *that*?"

"Well, not *me* and *Sally*, specifically," Michael interjected. "Just, you know, all interfaith couples."

"Oh, that's ridiculous," Bernice said, waving the back of her hand dismissively.

"I'm sorry, Bernice. I really just don't want to sit in temple for hours."

"Oh, really, dear—"

"I don't even know what the High Holy Days are all about."

"Well...it's the New Year."

I sighed, trying to breathe through my rising irritation. For years I had held my tongue about how pointless it seemed to me, observing a holiday that held no meaning to them. "What, exactly, is the difference between Rosh Hashanah and Yom Kippur?"

"Well, you know. It's when the New Year starts and the New Year ends," Michael explained.

I crossed my arms and legs, my foot tapping the table leg.

"And that's it? A long New Year?"

"It's actually our holiest time of year."

I was shocked to hear Amy's voice. Not only was she typically reserved in the company of four or more people, especially in the dominant presence of Bernice, but I had never heard Amy mention temple, services or anything remotely related to Judaism.

"When you're Jewish, if there is one time of year you go to temple, this is it," Amy said nonchalantly, reaching for the bowl of potato chips.

As I had figured, she didn't know a thing about the High Holy Days.

"Yeah, yeah. I've heard this before." I picked up Harrison's fork from the floor, setting it back at his place, where he resumed clanking it on the table. "But no one can explain *why* the holidays are so important."

"Well, on Rosh Hashanah, God opens the Book of Life and you take the time to review the past year. The times you were good to people, the times you were not. You look at all that you have done and what you could have done better." Amy brushed the crumbs from her palms. "For the next ten days, you're supposed to make right the wrongs."

"What do you mean, 'make right the wrongs'?" I asked suspiciously, recalling reciting ten empty Hail Marys during the one confessional I had memory of. A child of about seven years old, I had felt shrouded in shame, sitting in a wood booth, confessing my sins to a faceless voice on the other side of the mesh window. If I needed to apologize for something, shouldn't I own up to the error of my ways, looking a priest directly in the eye?

I pressed on with Amy. "You repent with prayer?"

"Well, yeah. Prayer is one way." Amy swept her hair from her forehead. "But, you're also supposed to get in touch with the people you may have hurt, or those you have neglected, and make it right with them. You call people, write letters…it's all about direct contact." She pressed her back to the wicker chair. "You have ten days to do this, because God is writing in the Book of Life for the next year. The book closes on Yom Kippur."

"What do you mean, 'the book closes'?"

"Well, supposedly, if you clean up everything from last year, God will write a good year for you ahead. Really, it's just a time when you can make a clean slate for yourself. Leave the past behind you and look ahead to the future."

I sat, stunned. Since childhood, I had always imagined the Divine as a forgiving entity, a sort of gentle, wise spirit. I had disliked the condemning and judgmental image given to God by the church. If what Amy said was true, Jews believed that the Divine was, indeed, compassionate. It was as if God said, "Yes, of course, you all make mistakes. Take this time to learn from them, reflecting on all you could have done better. Then, go to the people you have wronged and apologize. Make a promise to do better, and move on."

As a child, I was righteous in my feelings against confession. The priest seemed like an eavesdropper in his role as intermediary between God and me. I knew what I wanted to say, and I wanted to speak to God directly. After disclosing sins like hitting my sister or pilfering coins from my father's dresser, I was told to "do better" and to recite prayers for forgiveness, but I was never asked to apologize. I never felt that I actually repented for my sins.

Nor did I believe my sins were ever entirely forgiven. I

imagined the Divine carving tally marks on a weathered wood slab each time I teased my brother or gossiped about a friend, my chances for entering heaven diminishing with every lapse. The memory of my sins might soften with time, but the indelible marks of my behavior would never be erased. Worse, I never forgave myself. My mother always noted how hard I was on myself for forgetting my homework or being mean to my sister. It amazed me that Judaism offered the tools to be good to myself, to forgive myself, and to start fresh for a new year.

After years of presuming that Judaism had no spiritual depth, I found that the High Holy Days embodied convictions that, up until this point, I felt alone in espousing. I had always held that I needed to take responsibility for my wrongdoings and that in order to move forward, I had to make repairs. I believed in having conversations with God without a messenger. Most importantly, Judaism taught what I felt in the furthest reaches of my heart to be true: that God was forgiving.

I imagined how cleansed I would feel going into the autumn recognizing my shortcomings, with the chance to shed them before starting a new year. I would apologize to God for being stingy in my gratitude, often forgetting that my life was overflowing with incredible gifts like loving friends and family, my stylish apartment, my beautiful son. I would ask for forgiveness for the greed New York bred in me, giving me a false sense of need for the finer things in life. If I observed the High Holy Days, I would call my parents, confessing that I had neglected my Midwest roots, and I would thank them for their unshakable values that sustained me in the cutthroat business world of Manhattan.

"I had no idea...," I told Amy.

"Yeah, well...it's pretty cool."

I nodded, still absorbing the impact Amy's message had on me. Suddenly, everything I had known about Judaism seemed only the surface of something much deeper. I imagined holding a black, coarse ball in the palm of my hands, disappointed that it wasn't the crystal I had hoped it would be. Giving up on it, about to discard it, I suddenly discover a hairline crack, a bright light glowing in its center. Could it be there was actually something to this religion?

I pondered the idea of going to temple, but there was so much at stake. Not only did I feel excluded from Judaism; I felt somewhat of an outsider every day, a Wisconsin girl in Manhattan and the Hamptons. Now to risk what was most sacred to me — my spirituality — left me uncertain. Yet if attending temple could give me a better glimpse of that beautiful light, perhaps it was worth the risk.

But before I could respond to Amy and tell her that what she had said moved me, I heard Michael's voice. "Wow, soul-searching, reflecting *and* talking with people. You couldn't write a better religion for Sally."

A Second Visit

"Michael. Please. Could you check your pockets again?" Bernice implored, standing at the stairs of Central Synagogue.

It had been five years since I last walked through these doors. But now, after the inspiring discussion about the High Holy Days in the Hamptons, I wanted to give Judaism another chance. I was sure that my newfound optimism would erase the sting of the rabbi's words from my last experience at the temple.

That is, until I stood at the synagogue entrance. Now the rabbi's speech repeated in my ears as if I had heard it yesterday. "Parents, introduce your children to other Jews. Make it clear that interfaith marriage is unacceptable."

While Bernice fumbled for the tickets in her handbag, I couldn't shake the gnawing feeling that it would have been more prudent to read about Rosh Hashanah and Yom Kippur from the safe haven of my living room. In addition to having anxiety about hearing more slanderous remarks about non-Jews, I was starting to feel pangs of envy as I watched people file up the stairs. Sensing their inherent sense of belonging, I became acutely aware that I had none. Who was I kidding, thinking that this time would be any different? Nothing had changed. I was still a shiksa entering a Jewish temple.

As I entered the grand sanctuary, I looked for some mark of the passage of time as a symbol that things would be different this time. The cavernous room, still impressive by any architectural standards, echoed with the hum of people talking over one another, a sea of crisp suits and designer dresses. It was exactly as it had been five years earlier.

Once again I felt alien as we climbed up the narrow stairs to the balcony, just as we had years before. When I was a young girl, the solemn sound of the organ lured me into the asylum of the church. I longed now to hear heavy-chorded hymns, to be transported back to my childhood when I walked amongst my seven family members and entered the fold of our friends. How lovely it would be to step into a room of welcoming faces. The feeling of instantaneous acceptance, of belonging, seemed a vague memory.

"There," Michael pointed. "There are three seats."

Approaching the same section of pews I had sat in last time, an acute sense of missing Harrison came over me. Although he was typically happy with our sitter, irrational thoughts paraded through my mind. Harrison howling uncontrollably in Hazel's dimpled arms, face red and wet from tears, hands reaching for a mommy not there. Harrison choking on a Cheerio, Hazel panicking, forgetting to call 911. I was accustomed to being away from my son but never comfortable with it. Now, standing at the entrance to the pew, I wanted to turn on my heel and go to where I was needed, where I was indispensable in someone's life. Where I knew I was missed at this very moment.

Michael handed me a prayer book. "Did you tell Hazel what time we'd be back?"

"Yes. She's meeting us at your mother's building so we can take Harrison to lunch after this." I had discussed this several times with Michael.

"Oh, good."

"Michael," Bernice leaned over across me. "You're not going back to work, are you?"

"No, mother. We're going to lunch with you, remember?"

"You know," she said, enrolling me, "he really shouldn't go back to work."

I smiled and nodded. When the organ music swelled in minor

key, filling the synagogue, I suppressed my instinct to stand, as we always had when the priest walked down the aisle, surprised that I still felt the impulse after all these years.

The procession of rabbis and board members stirred little interest in my row. As they strode down the center aisle, the white yarmulkes floating toward the bema, I peered over the balcony, wondering again who all the people accompanying the clergy were.

"Do you know any of those people?" I whispered to Michael.

"No," he whispered back. "But my mom knows the rabbi."

What did he mean that Bernice "knew" the rabbi? Did that mean she would drop by for a chat on Wednesday afternoon, like my mother stopped by the rectory to talk with the priests? Did Bernice go to the rabbi when she needed advice, during times of inner conflict? I had no idea. Unlike my mother, who sparred about Bible passages with the priests over dinner at our house or discussed theology around the campfire with friends on church campouts, Bernice never discussed God or her spirituality. In fact, aside from the High Holy Days, she never even mentioned the synagogue. I couldn't imagine my mother-in-law consulting with a rabbi. In this congregation of thousands, how would the rabbi know her?

As the clergy and its members settled into their seats and the cantor poised at the podium to sing his first song, a flurry of questions engulfed me. What is the cantor singing? Do most Jewish people understand Hebrew? I knew Michael and his family did not, evident by the clumsy Hebrew passages at Seder. But what about the majority of Reform Jews? Does the cantor sing the same opening song every Rosh Hashanah? How does one become a cantor? Do cantors undergo rigorous rabbinic training and decide to sing instead? Or is a cantor simply a singer who happens to like Hebrew?

Michael passed a prayer book to me and to his mother. I read the title framed by a gold rectangle, *Gates of Repentance*, and noted how the mixture of font and color created a somber and distinguished tone. I opened the book, realized I was looking at the last page, flipped it over and started at page one, the subtitle, *The New Union Prayerbook for the Days of Awe*, stirring more questions. Who wrote this prayer book? Do temples across the country, throughout the world, use the same book? Is it an ancient text or was it written this century? What, exactly, comprises the Union? Was this a New York edition?

I rolled the pages left to right, past notes on the usage of the book and half a dozen pages of acknowledgements. My fingers stopped on page three, *Meditations*.

Meditations? Judaism has meditations? This was incredible. During my mother's journey in search of a new faith, she had discovered meditation and briefly tried to enroll her children in the practice. I had liked guided meditations, discovering them a useful tool for coping with stress and finding peace in times of career changes and other uncertainties. But I hadn't been able to stay focused with Vipasana meditation, paying attention to my breath while letting thoughts come and go. I found myself instead drawn to books offering daily meditations, positive thoughts for the day. I had no idea that a religion steeped in ancient tradition could embrace such a spiritual practice. How had I missed these meditations last time?

Yet there was the word on the top of page three: *Meditations.* Would we be reading these meditations in unison during the service? Was it considered rude to read them silently to oneself? The cantor's voice crooned above me as I read the sentences directly under Number One.

Just as the hand, held before the eye, can hide the tallest mountain, so the routine of everyday life can keep us from seeing the vast radiance and the secret wonders of the world.
—Chasidic, 18th century

This was exactly the issue I had been struggling with lately, being present to the everyday gifts. So often I hurried through the streets of Manhattan, caught up in my own thoughts, ignoring the city's history, the mix of architecture, the energy. I read the meditation again. It was so typical of me to carry a constant dialogue in my head, going over my list of things to do, people to call, ruminating on a disagreement with Michael, deciding what to make for dinner, that seldom did I slow down to appreciate that my dream had come true — my childhood dream — of living and working in New York City.

And now I had even more: a loving husband and an adorable son. How often did I slow down enough to appreciate these gifts?

My eyes hungrily scanned the next few paragraphs looking for another gem. Many of the proverbs made reference to the Torah or used Hebrew words, making them fall flat in meaning for me. I stopped on number 22.

If you see a friend sinning...it is a Mitzvah to try to restore that person to the right path. Let your friend know that wrong actions are self-inflicted hurts, but speak softly and gently, making it clear that you speak only because of your concern for your friend's well-being.

—Maimonides, 12th century

I couldn't believe this! Judaism gives permission to interfere in someone's life? Yet following the simple instruction on how to intervene nicely, one's interference actually becomes a selfless act of love. In my family, we never confronted each other with concerns about wrongdoings. However, we felt quite comfortable talking *about* one another, a practice that continued into the present.

I wondered what it might be like to be part of a culture where one expected to receive unsolicited guidance from others. My father took pride in the fact that he never meddled in his adult children's affairs. "You are always my children to me, but I know better than to interfere in your lives." While I deeply appreciated that my parents didn't pressure me to live to any high standard, reading the meditation identified a longing of mine — to have wisdom imparted to me now and then.

When I had taken a hiatus from college to attend a two-year school, following a boyfriend to a small town, it would have been helpful if my mother had sat me down and told me what I was sacrificing by transferring schools. When I moved from one job to the next in New York, feeling aimless and unfocused, a show of concern from my father could have helped me. Having worked in the Milwaukee public school system for most of his career, his perspective on career stability and enduring difficult times in a job would have been infinitely valuable.

I thought, too, of how I could have helped others along their journeys. When my college roommate was dating a drug user, rather than make comments to her that he had huge personal problems, I could have lovingly sat with her and told her of my concerns for her well-being. According to Judaism, doing so was not an invasion of privacy — it was Jewish law. It reminded me that we are all responsible for one another, that we all have something at stake in each other's welfare.

I was getting excited. I might not know what was going on in the ritual of the service, but the meditations reached out and pulled me deeper into myself. Reading number 20, which described the great care we must take not to shame people, I felt validated. My mother and father had a habit of telling embarrassing stories about their children, usually at a dinner party. "Did you know Sally thought Alaska was an island till she was in high school?" When I finally told my parents of my hurt feelings, they brushed me off for being too sensitive.

I felt more and more electrified as I continued reading the meditations. Number 24 spoke of how to embrace life; 25, of how to lead an ethical life; 30, of accepting that we all are but a balance of merits and faults. My excitement burgeoned, as it had when Amy first explained the significance of the High Holy Days.

This was Judaism? Why hadn't anyone told me?

"Pssst! Honey!" I whispered to Michael, barely able to contain myself. "Did you see these?"

He peered at my page number, perplexed, then shook his head, pointing to his page.

The cantor returned to his seat. I placed my finger between the pages of the meditations, turning my attention to the bema.

"Page 82," announced the rabbi, now standing at the pulpit.

I joined the congregation in Psalm 15, our recitations suddenly clear and meaningful.

Eternal God, who may abide in Your house? Who may dwell in Your holy mountain? Those who are upright; who do justly; who speak the truth within their hearts...

Together, more than a thousand people declared that to stand in God's House, we must not exploit others, and we must speak the truth. How refreshingly specific!

...who do not slander others or wrong them or bring shame upon them.

I remembered being shocked at the amount of backstabbing on Seventh Avenue, co-workers gossiping about one another in the break room, in the cubicles, even after hours. I tried my best to tune it out or to steer the conversations to another topic. A work peer once told another manager, "Don't talk to Sally about this — she won't say anything bad." It was a reputation I was proud of, allowing me to maintain a positive attitude at work. When I did engage in gossip, I felt it in my gut afterward, my body reminding me I had betrayed others.

I turned my attention back to the service. The congregation

read on about the miracles of daily life, the text beseeching us to
take notice of all that is before us, and to give strength to those
around us. This notion was just as compelling at the meditations I
read to myself. I thought about how much better life seemed
when I stepped outside of my inner dialogue and paid attention
to my surroundings. When I did so, I found it easier to reach out
as well, particularly to my family. My siblings and parents had
been a source of strength for me from the moment I decided to
move to Manhattan, a resource on which I could depend in times
of wavering confidence. "You can do it, Sal" — words from my
brothers and sisters, popped into my mind often.

At times, the congregation read phrases about being a Jew and
crowning Israel, neither of which I could relate to, but I was able
to bypass them, looking forward to the next portion of the service
where I hoped to glean more soulful sentiment from the passages.

How had I not noticed the poignancy of the service five years
before? Perhaps I had been so overwhelmed by my first
experience in a temple, I was incapable of paying attention to the
thrust of the service. Jarred by the lack of crucifix, the
overwhelming amount of Hebrew, the backwards book, even the
music in minor key, there had been a lot to take in. Now, perched
above the main sanctuary in Central Synagogue, I followed a
service that talked of revering God, leading a balanced life, and
taking ownership of our actions. Whenever the cantor sang, I
flipped back to the meditative readings, understanding now how
Gregorian chanting stimulates introspection. The lilting lyrics in
another language released me from obligation to listen astutely,
providing instead the perfect background music to enter my own
mind. I was at peace, and I enjoyed the time to simply think and
reflect. Closing my eyes, I took in the presence of my family. I felt
the love of my husband, who adored me despite my quirks and
shortcomings. How often had he wrapped his arms around me
when I felt lost or aimless, giving me sanctuary in his embrace? I
felt the love and acceptance of my Jewish mother-in-law. Never

had she asked me to convert or change a thing about myself. She accepted her daughter-in-law, the Catholic girl from Wisconsin. Here, within the mass of people in the cavernous synagogue, I felt my home in the family beside me.

I opened my eyes to see two people sliding aside the doors of the ark, removing the Torah. The congregation, which suddenly did not seem so alien, stood, bent briefly at the knees in reverence, and took their seats to listen to the readings. As I watched various congregants chant portions from the Torah in Hebrew, the questions piled up like a pyramid of bricks needing mortar. *Why were these people selected to read? Did they really know and understand Hebrew? What do the words in the scroll look like?* Suddenly, the most critical question struck me: *If I'm asking all of these questions, does it mean I am actually interested in aspects of this religion?*

Since moving to Manhattan, I had dabbled in exploring different faiths. My visits to the Science of Mind and the Unitarian Universalist churches were gratifying, but only momentarily. More and more, I felt a need for a lasting sense of belonging. As motherhood became more demanding and the importance of nurturing my spirituality became more pronounced, my craving for a religion and a community that reflected my beliefs became stronger.

Five years ago, sitting in this very temple, Judaism topped my list of unfeasible faiths. Not only did I understand Judaism to lack any spirituality, I was blatantly shut out from joining its members. Even though that service had shocked and offended me, I experienced a small sense of relief. My identity as non-Jew suited me perfectly. I could be married to a Jewish man, promise to honor his religion when raising our children, but still buy a Christmas tree and attend the Fifth Avenue Easter Parade. I could embrace the warmth of my new Jewish family, be accepted fully by them, but still identify with my brothers and sisters. Although I had married a Jewish man, adding a sort of exotic flair to our family dynamic, I hadn't personally adopted his religion and was therefore still "one of them."

Yet, if I had the perfect position in my Jewish family, a formerly Catholic girl wanting only to better understand Judaism, why were questions about Judaism plaguing me? Was it possible this religion actually touched me? Somewhere between the meaningful meditations and the mystical music, was I actually thinking Judaism could be a foundation for my own spirituality?

Finally, with the Torah covered and returned to the ark, we closed our books and the rabbi approached the bema.

"L'shana tova."

"L'shana tova," we answered.

A wave of nervousness washed over me as I waited for the rabbi's message, the comfort I'd felt from the readings suddenly gone, like a fickle friend. I swallowed hard, my tongue searching for saliva to replenish my mouth that had become a dry riverbed. I suddenly felt foolish. In the last two hours, I had embraced parts of Jewish thinking I hadn't known existed, sound bites that enticed me. They now seemed like delicate nuggets of hope. I felt a precarious optimism that Judaism might have some significance for me. It wasn't that I was considering converting, but maybe there was something to garner from this religion, some soulful substance I could impart to our children. I romanced the idea of keeping the door to Judaism open. Since it was Michael's religion, and would soon be Harrison's, perhaps there might be something meaningful in it for me.

Now, the rabbi standing before me — the same man who had declared that Jews should only marry Jews and urged parents to orchestrate such arrangements — had the singular power to shatter my newfound sparkle of hope. Suddenly, I felt like a silly jilted girlfriend approaching the boy who had snubbed her repeatedly, holding onto the fantasy that he'd had a reversal of heart. What could I possibly have been thinking? One rabbi at the 92nd Street Y had made it absolutely clear that he was against interfaith marriage. This very rabbi I was about to listen to had renounced interfaith marriage even more vehemently. Yet I inexplicably returned willingly to his synagogue, delusional enough to think he might have changed his way of thinking. Worse, I had tossed caution aside, allowing myself to become caught up in meditations and text.

I couldn't know what the rabbi was going to preach, but I expected the worst. I quickly looked for a mental escape route. Perhaps I could read from the prayer book again, seeking sanction and inspiration from the meditations. But I knew the rabbi's booming voice would override my ability to focus on the text. I could simply daydream or concoct lists of things to do, but ultimately I came to the conclusion that there would be no cognitive escape.

However, I could physically remove myself. As the rabbi cleared his throat, I decided that this time I would not sit through a talk that offended me. I looked to my left, calculating how many pairs of knees I would have to crawl over to depart. It would cause a stir for a moment, but I could whisper to Michael to meet me outside after the service, and I would be gone.

"It is not often that we sit together as a congregation, to come together to praise God."

There was a rustling in the crowd, perhaps of guilt. If the mass of people in the sanctuary were anything like most Reform Jews I knew, I assumed they never attended synagogue on the Sabbath.

"As Jews, we know that we practice our faith in our homes, in our families, and in our communities. Yet, I must ask myself, 'Why is it that we are not compelled to attend services on the Sabbath?'"

I had a rush of feeling simpatico with the rabbi. For years, the fact that Reform Jews rarely attended weekly services had been a matter of concern for me. How was it, I wondered, that Jewish people felt no need to attend Sabbath services, yet still considered themselves devout Jews? But I caught myself, remembering that my trust in the rabbi had been demolished before a foundation was even built, and I held tight to my wariness.

"What is it that keeps us from our synagogue?'"

I wasn't sure where the rabbi was going with this, but I knew he wasn't going to talk my in-laws into going to services every Friday night.

"What is it that makes us Jewish?"

The rabbi's question echoed my most profound confusion about Judaism. For all of my Passovers, Hanukkahs, and conversations with friends, I could still not get a clear idea of what being Jewish meant to people.

"Is being Jewish about our faith? Our traditions? Our history? Or is it our belief in God?"

Exactly! I thought. I wanted to point at the rabbi and nod to others in validation. *This is what I've been saying!*

The rabbi paused, his eyes scanning the congregation. "My answer is 'yes.'"

I leaned forward, puzzled. My inner dialogue stopped.

"For there are many ways in which one can be Jewish. There is Judaism the faith. There is Judaism the heritage. And both are valid reasons for being Jewish."

All sound ceased for me at that moment. There was no rustling in the pews or echoes of coughs. All color, all objects and shapes disappeared, too. For the first time, someone had made a distinction that no one had been able to make for me. Time and again I had asked Jewish people what being Jewish meant to them, only to be answered with blank stares. Some said they weren't even sure they believed in God. How was it, I wondered, that they could be part of a religion without believing in God? Wasn't that a contradiction?

I had also wondered how one could suddenly consider themselves Jewish by the mere act of converting. I had the same quandary after living in New York for several years. Had I lived there long enough to call myself a New Yorker? Judaism was deeply imbued with ritual, tradition and heritage. It seemed preposterous for one to simply declare oneself Jewish and expect to feel part of that.

A few years earlier, after a friend of mine had converted, I couldn't wait to sit her down for dinner and ask her pointed — bordering on rude — questions.

"So, what do you tell people when they ask you what religion you are?"

"I tell them I'm Jewish."

"Just like that? You don't tell them you used to be Catholic and you converted to Judaism?"

"No, because I'm not Catholic. I'm Jewish."

I had been utterly perplexed. How could she suddenly declare herself to be Jewish? It would be like one day deciding I'm Irish.

Up to this point, when imagining someone converting to Judaism, I envisioned a parade of Jews walking down a street in Israel, full, white cloaks caught in the breeze and the convert trying to catch up to them, reaching to catch hold of their flapping fabric. "Wait for me!" the convert would call after them, panting. "I want to be part of you!"

The rabbi's statement helped me understand why Jewish text that spoke of "our people" left me feeling alienated. Judaism is a heritage, and I simply couldn't pretend I was part of it. The mere thought of it made me feel like an imposter — my lineage was Croatian and French Canadian, with a little Prussian. My ancestors were not Jewish and never would be.

Yet, as the rabbi described it, I *could* consider myself Jewish one day because, separate from the heritage, there was also Judaism as a religion. I wouldn't have to pretend to know how to make brisket or be familiar with the rituals around holidays. I could learn about the religion, believe in its tenets and be accepted as a Jew. The beliefs, which were starting to resonate with me, could be the foundation for my spirituality. I didn't have to be part of the tribe to be Jewish.

Now I could stop judging my Jewish friends who saw only the value in their heritage. Their form of Judaism — attending the High Holy Day services, hosting Break Fast dinners, gathering for holiday celebrations, getting married under a huppa — was as valid as my embracing the religion.

By the time the rabbi finished his sermon, I knew I wanted to learn more about Judaism. With the meditations, the text and the rabbi's explanation of Jewishness, my objections were falling away.

"And now," the rabbi closed the service, "at the beginning of a New Year, we pray for blessing: the spirit of wisdom and understanding, the spirit of insight and courage, the spirit of knowledge and reverence; may we overcome trouble, pain and sorrow..."

With each word, I felt as if my own father were sending me off into the world with years of wisdom, experience and love behind his words.

"Eternal God and God of our people, renew us for a good year." With these final words, we were sent off to start our ten days of reflection and healing.

As I walked out of the temple, I stood for a moment on the steps, throngs of congregants scurrying past me, their arms raised to hail cabs at the curb. The rabbi's words still echoed in my head. A person could be Jewish without a belief in God or an understanding of Judaism's tenets—their heritage was enough. On the other hand, a person could be Jewish by living the principles of Judaism without being part of the ancestry. One did not have to be both.

Tilting my head up to the bright, autumn sun, I thought, *It is, indeed, a New Year.*

The Welcome

"Hello. Larchmont Temple."

The receptionist answered on the first ring, making it impossible for me to hang up, an urge I'd been suppressing since first dialing.

"Oh, yes. Hello. I'm interested in making an appointment with the rabbi. Is that possible? Is that, uh, something he does?"

"Sure," the voice answered in a brogue. I was perplexed, wondering if there were Jews in Scotland. "I'll connect you to his assistant."

Deciding that Scottish Jews probably were not that commonplace, I wondered what had led the receptionist to work at a temple. A vague surge of comfort followed; maybe a non-Jew in the temple was not so peculiar. I leaned against the kitchen counter, waiting to be connected to the next voice, letting this soothing thought seek its place in my mind.

"Hello, this is Cynthia." A mousey, middle-aged voice spoke.

"Oh, hi. I'm calling to set up an appointment with the rabbi?" In my nervousness, my voice returned to its annoying Midwest inflection — ending sentences with a rise in the voice, as if all statements were questions. I sounded like a Milwaukee waitress. *"Hello? My name is Marge? I'll be your server for the evening?"*

"Okay," Cynthia continued. "Are you a member?"

I paused, fiddling with a pencil on the counter.

"No, I'm not."

"What is this regarding?"

"Um, I guess conversion." I imagined Cynthia writing CONVERSION in block letters in the rabbi's desk calendar. "Well, not really *conversion*. I'm just interested in Judaism, and we're moving to the area soon and our real-estate broker suggested I call. That you would be a good temple to call."

I heard the sound of pages flipping.

"So, um, I'm calling."

"Okay…how is Thursday, 9:30?"

"Nine-thirty? That's fine. Great." I felt like a teenager accepting a date with someone I wasn't sure I actually wanted to go out with.

Scheduling my first appointment with a rabbi was as easy as that.

***

It had been a summer of momentous change. Michael and I had moved our family out of the city, trading the crowded Upper West Side of Manhattan for the idyllic life of Larchmont. It was precisely the environment I wanted to raise our children in — a sleepy Westchester suburb that boasted traditional family life and an outstanding school system. With our four-room Manhattan apartment sold and our new house undergoing renovations, we had rented a home in Westchester for six months. A week after moving in, I took a pregnancy test and discovered why I had been feeling tired and nauseous —our second child was on the way. With all these transitions happening at once, more than ever I yearned for some stability, a spiritual structure that would help me feel grounded. Thursday's appointment with the rabbi arrived before I knew it.

"What are you going to ask him?" Michael stood next to me as I packed Harrison's diaper bag for the babysitter. I paused and shrugged my shoulders.

"I don't know."

"Are you going to tell him you want to convert?"

"No. I don't know if I want to convert." I slid a packet of powdered formula into a side pouch. It struck me that the black quilted diaper bag looked too metropolitan for our quaint suburb. "I really don't know what to expect."

"You don't?"

"Well, no. Maybe you can tell me what it's like to meet with a rabbi."

Michael jerked back his head defensively. "*I* don't know."

"Well, are rabbis typically intimidating?"

"I dunno."

"Will he care that I'm not Jewish?"

"I don't know, I keep telling you."

"Well, why don't you know?" I couldn't understand why Michael was being so cryptic in his responses.

"I've never met with a rabbi before," he replied, looking at me as if I were asking if he had met with the mayor's Anti-Graffiti Task Force or something equally out of left field.

"In all your years at Central Synagogue, you've never met with a rabbi?"

This was incredible to me. When I was growing up, the clergy were very much a part of my family's lives. Father Joe, the youngest priest, often jogged up through the grassy backyards from the rectory seven houses away, stopping to push us on our swing before visiting our mom, often staying for dinner. We kids thought nothing of knocking on the rectory door just to say hi, sometimes bringing a gift of lemonade or cookies. The priests even camped out with parish families on weekend trips, something I thought remarkable at the time. After all, what would priests talk about to adults, outside of church?

We were so intimate with the clergy that I had a private First Communion at our home, with Father Joe officiating. Feeling like a princess in a lacy white dress, veil and white gloves, I took my first sacrament surrounded by aunts, uncles and cousins in the warm surroundings of my home. Guests sat on the two loveseats my mother had reupholstered in crushed green velvet, setting their drinks on the glass mosaic tables my parents had pieced together by hand, and tapped on the keys of the baby grand piano in the corner. Since the living room was typically off limits to children, taking my first communion there was symbolic of assuming my place with the grown-ups in the Catholic Church.

Now I stood in our kitchen, clutching the diaper bag of a child who would be raised Jewish, about to embark on my own Jewish odyssey, discovering that my husband was even more removed from his religion than I'd imagined.

"You mean to tell me that you've never been in a rabbi's office?"

"Just to meet with him a couple of times before my bar mitzvah. But I don't remember much about it."

I sighed. Knowing that a bar mitzvah requires intense study, I had imagined Michael meeting with his rabbi, asking questions, refuting theories, discussing assignments.

All of my teen and adult life, I had the confidence I could handle any encounter, given the right preparation. From addressing hundreds of people in school assemblies and seminars to presenting clothing lines at retail meetings, I always had success because I had studied, researched and rehearsed. Now, my primary source of information — Michael — offered me absolutely no insight into Judaism. I would be entering a rabbi's office for the very first time with only Catholic references to fall back on. I felt like I was on a ship, about to enter the port of an uncharted island, uncertain if the natives would welcome or repel me. This was to be my personal journey.

***

I was excited at the prospect of learning the blueprint of a new community. The relocation bug had hooked me years ago. After I moved away to college, I thrived on change, accepting a summer internship in Chicago, studying abroad in London, spending summer vacation in Colorado. I moved to Manhattan days after graduation and lived in several different communities in New York, Hoboken and Long Island. Nothing could replace the exhilaration of experiencing things for the first time, or the confidence gained from making a new neighborhood my home. Now, here I was, pregnant with my second child, driving through a beautiful suburb, about to meet with a rabbi. I could feel the pulse of transformation with every turn of the steering wheel.

It came as no surprise to me that Norman Rockwell had lived part of his childhood in this section of Westchester. Surely his paintings must have been inspired by the tree-lined streets, the charming storefronts and the corner ice-cream shop. I drove through the business district, eyes scanning the clothing boutiques, the headless mannequins posed mid-action, and restaurants with windows framed in velvet drapes. I made a mental note of delis with stools tucked under the counters, imagining sharing a sandwich with Harrison in the near future, and wondered if the bookstore a few doors down had a good children's selection. At the end of the retail division, a bustling intersection at Boston Post Road, I spotted a synagogue with a carved menorah above its corner entrance. With just two steps up to the single door, the entrance was humble and unassuming. I crossed the intersection, peering through my car window, looking for the entrance to the parking lot, until I read *Beth Emeth* carved in the stone above the doorway. I was surprised to find another temple and wondered why my realtor hadn't mentioned Beth Emeth as an option. *How would I know if I was choosing the right temple? Would this be the first of many rabbinic interviews?*

With the business district behind me and only a mile or so until I plunged into the Long Island Sound, I drove slowly, certain that I had inadvertently passed Larchmont Temple. I looked at my watch and decided to go a few blocks further before retracing my route. I passed the public library, the quarter-acre of green shrubs in front creating the quintessential image of a small-town library; the French-American School, its blond brick tower centered on a wall of tall paned glass windows; and a flat, green park, with walking paths and gazebo. Finally, several blocks past Boston Post Road, I found the address that matched the one scrawled in the notebook that lay open on the passenger seat.

Surrounded by lush oak trees and a slender strip of lawn, the entrance of the auburn brick building was framed by white columns and a triangular cornice, creating a modest but stately portico. If I had driven any faster, I would have missed it, mistaking it for a bank. No stained-glass windows peeked through the mass of trees lining the front wall; no religious symbol adorned the entry. Only the words "Larchmont Temple" etched discreetly above the double doors gave me the tip-off that I had reached my destination.

I parked the car across the street and crossed the quiet avenue. Bypassing the stately doors, remembering the instructions to use the side entrance, I descended a few concrete steps, pulled open the white, paneled door and stepped into the gray-carpeted entry of the administrative offices. I inhaled, sniffing something vaguely familiar. Whenever I had walked into the foyer of Our Lady of Lourdes, the still, quiet atmosphere enveloped me, and the echo of my steps on the marble floors made me feel conspicuous. The lights were always dimmed, forcing me to stand still for half a minute while my pupils adjusted to the darkness.

My experience in Larchmont Temple was the opposite. There was an energy throbbing in this space below the sanctuary. It was full of life and activity — keyboards clicking, copy machines whirring, metal file drawers rolling shut and rattling their frames, phones ringing, women talking. I glanced to my left, following the source of commotion. About half a dozen desks abutted the walls of the brightly lit office, where three women moved about. I approached the threshold apprehensively.

"Hello?"

A woman looked up from her desk. "Yes, hello!" I immediately recognized her Scottish accent.

"I have an appointment with Rabbi Sirkman. Can you tell me where I should go?"

A second woman at the furthermost desk called out. "Hi." She peered from behind her glasses. "Are you Sally?"

"Yes, I am."

"You can have a seat outside. The rabbi will be right with you."

Two mismatched office chairs in the corridor around the corner faced a bulletin board. Within moments of selecting a seat, I jumped to my feet again, too antsy to sit. I took a few steps and popped my head into an open doorway, discovering a small, worn library, books scattered on the dented, bulky table in the center of the room, the shelves scrambled.

Afraid I'd be caught in a place I didn't belong, I turned back to the bulletin board and eyed the various colored flyers — a bright green 8 ½ x 11 paper announced a Brotherhood breakfast featuring a guest speaker, a Jewish author. A Caring Community flyer, in bold pink, offered rides to temple for nondrivers and healing tapes from the library. Women of Reform Judaism was hosting a High Holy Days crafts class. A religious-school calendar listed various Jewish holidays I had never heard of; and a Torah Study schedule was posted, listing Torah portions with corresponding dates.

The number of unfamiliar words on the postings overwhelmed me. It was as if the fliers mocked me, reminding me that I had entered foreign territory. In addition to the Hebrew-language barrier, I could see I would have to overcome a culture obstacle. I couldn't imagine why there were so many sub-groups of people. Although my family had been very active in the church, I had no recollection of any sub-populations in Our Lady of Lourdes. We were all simply congregants. We attended services every Sunday, we maintained relationships with the clergy, we socialized at church and outside of the weekly services, and that was about it. As a child, I was unaware of any committee work my parents participated in. Now, looking around the catacombs of the temple, hearing the sounds of a busy office next to me, imagining numerous communities of people under one roof, life at Larchmont Temple seemed unruly. More important, how would I ever understand all of this?

As I stepped away from the bulletin board, a shadow exiting the office caught my attention.

"Hello there!"

I turned to see a dark-haired man lumber toward me. He was in his early forties, with the enthusiastic tone of a college kid on the pep squad. I discerned a Boston accent.

"I'm Rabbi Sirkman." He looked straight through his spectacles and into my eyes, seeming absolutely delighted to see me. It was as if we were old friends about to sit down and reminisce about our high school years. I reached for his extended hand.

"Hi. I'm Sally."

"Hi there! I'm so glad you could be here!" The rabbi waved his hand toward his hip. "C'mon in. Let's talk."

I was happy to follow behind him so I could conceal my surprise at his age. I hadn't expected my prospective spiritual teacher to be only a few years older than me, or just a few inches taller. There was nothing stereotypically rabbinic about this man walking in front of me. His suit looked tailored — a European cut, I noted by the jacket without a back vent. His haircut was contemporary, brushed forward and to the side over his brow, and his round, wire-rimmed glasses were of the style displayed in the Upper West Side eyeglass boutiques. It's not that I expected a rabbi to be dressed in the cloaks worn at services, but I imagined someone similar to most of the priests I was raised among — stodgy, slow-moving older men who had little zest for their work.

"C'mon in. Have a seat." Rabbi Sirkman scooped papers off the cushion of a worn tweed loveseat, dropping them on the coffee table. I sat down and took in another set of new surroundings. Floor-to-ceiling bookcases bursting with volumes — some aligned neatly, others piled haphazardly — covered the walls behind me and to my left. Across from me, behind the rabbi's desk, a window looked out from below street level, the view of passing feet obscured by the stacks of books that cluttered the windowsill. And to my right, a ledge that ran the length of the wall displayed artwork and more photographs.

"So! It's so nice to meet you!" the rabbi enthused.

"Thank you. It's really nice to be here." I nodded, smiling broadly, realizing my words were true. Having moved to Westchester just a month ago, I had gone from the vibrant environment of urban life to the stillness and isolation of life in suburbia. Every morning I drove Michael to the commuter train and returned to our rental house, located on a busy strip, where I knew no one. It felt wonderful to be in the company of someone who seemed genuinely glad to see me.

Sitting in this office, enveloped by a friendly, welcoming force, surrounded by symbols of potential knowledge, I suddenly felt safe and at home. My entire body relaxed, and I found myself slinging one elbow over the back of the loveseat

"So, Sally! Tell me why you're here! What can I do for you?"

I had expected to tell the rabbi my geographic history, how I had moved from Manhattan to Westchester, finding the temple based on location and a realtor's recommendation. Instead, I threw myself into the story of my spiritual quest.

"I have been looking for a religious home for quite some time." I spoke slowly, feeling the weight of the story in my words. "The world around me...it's filled with *such* beauty. I look at the swaying trees, the leaves fluttering in the wind, and I'm in awe of God's gifts. I'm so lucky to be able to witness these gifts every day." Tears filled my eyes. "I can't believe I'm crying. I'm sorry."

The rabbi smiled. "No! Tears are good! Go on!"

"Well, it's just that God is so present in my life every day. I was once asked if I pray. I'm always praying. It's as if I'm in a continuous conversation with God."

The rabbi leaned forward, his forearms on his knees, smiling and nodding. I laughed, relieved to be accepted despite my swelling emotion.

"Now, I've got one child, one on the way, and as wonderful as life is, I still feel like there is a piece of me missing. I really want to find a spiritual home, a place — well, a place where I can be more of who I am."

The rabbi tossed his hands in the air, smiling even more broadly. "That sounds wonderful! So, here you are. I take it you weren't raised Jewish."

"Oh, no! I'm just learning about Judaism now, and quite frankly, it has me confused." Realizing I hadn't answered the rabbi's question, I continued. "I was raised Catholic, but found a long time ago that that faith just doesn't fit me."

My journey to the rabbi's office suddenly seemed too complex to recap in one meeting. While the church had been a prominent part of my upbringing, after a more truthful reflection on my childhood, I realized it was the community of the congregation that I had thrived on, not the theology of Catholicism. When my parents were excluded from the church social group after their divorce, I was secretly devastated. I missed the sense of belonging I had at Our Lady of Lourdes.

After my parents were shut out from the church, my mother set out on her own to find a fulfilling spiritual home. I enthusiastically joined her in her exploration of alternative religions. I felt adventurous and so different from my high school friends, all of whom attended traditional houses of worship. My mother and I swayed and sang loudly in a Baptist church, clapping along and singing the praises of God. We took in the sermons at the Unitarian Universalist Church that preached acceptance of all individuals, and we purchased books in the lobby. At Science of Mind services, we embraced the upbeat, positive look at God, awed by all the good the Divine can do for the lives of people. By the time I had moved to New York, my mom had introduced broad concepts of spirituality to me through books on meditation, positive thinking and more.

My spirituality took a back seat to the excitement of Manhattan. Sunday morning brunches and museums replaced church, and striving for a lucrative career took my focus from religion. Yet the more I became settled into a routine of work and dating Michael, the more I found myself missing a sense of spirituality in my life. Attending services in New York at Science of Mind and the Unitarian Universalist Church brought me inspired teachings, but I was still lacking a profound sense of belonging.

I placed my palms over my stomach. "Now, here I am, expecting our second baby, wanting a religion that reflects my beliefs. I know it sounds hokey, but it's the bottom-line truth."

"That's not hokey — that's wonderful!" The rabbi's enthusiasm was reassuring. "Was your husband raised Jewish?"

"Well, yes, but he's not the reason I'm here. I mean, I know about Judaism because of Michael. But he couldn't tell me much about it. It's been so frustrating!"

"Michael's level of knowledge about Judaism is very common," the rabbi assured me. "I'm guessing he went to Hebrew school, hated it, had his bar mitzvah and that's where his Jewish education ended."

"Exactly! How did you know?"

"Because that's how it usually went with people in his generation. It's a shame." He shook his head. "It's why we work so hard to make Jewish education fun for kids today."

"I really have no idea what being Jewish is. It's overwhelming... and I keep hitting dead ends in trying to understand it. I had given up hope."

"What do you mean, 'dead ends'?"

I went on to describe the 92nd Street Y class, my experience with the High Holy Days services many years ago, and conversations with Jews who knew little about their theology.

"Well, I am sorry you experienced that class and the *d'var Torah* at the synagogue. I wish that could be changed."

"But," I continued, "I recently found out what the High Holy Days are about, and, well, I'm just stunned." I scooted forward on the cushion, eager to tell him of my revelation. "The idea of a fresh start, of a clean slate every year. And to make amends with *people*, not only with God… it just makes sense." I grinned, unabashed. "And I have to wonder, what else does this religion hold?"

As I described my anticipation, the rabbi nodded and walked around the coffee table to the bookshelves behind me, scanning the hundreds of spines. I turned to watch him.

"… so I'm not sure, really, where to begin to learn. Do I take a class? Do I study the Torah?"

"Let's start here." He pulled a bright orange soft-cover book from the third shelf. "Take this book." I held the book in my hands, reading the title *To Life!* by Harold Kushner. How he had located the title immediately amongst all the books on the shelves was beyond my comprehension.

"Take it? Oh, no. I couldn't take it. I'll just get my own." Always apprehensive about borrowing books, afraid I'll misplace or simply forget to return them, I certainly was not going to borrow a *rabbi's* book. What if I lost it, or spilled coffee on it, or dropped it in a puddle? This could be a very bad start to my first relationship with a rabbi.

"No, no, take it! When you're ready to mark up your own, you'll bring this back."

*****

The pages of *To Life!* seemed to turn themselves. My excitement was evidenced by my pen sailing feverishly through my composition notebook. I was a bottomless well of questions, revelations and exclamations. Harold Kushner stated the tenets of Judaism clearly, sometimes contrasting the religion to Christianity. As I absorbed each principle, it was as if a spotlight shone down on the pages. Here, in the text of *To Life!*, my own beliefs were validated and my ideas were broadened.

I read that Judaism believes we are responsible for our behavior, for what we *do*, not what we think, dream or fantasize about. Growing up in a Catholic home, I constantly edited my thoughts, not wanting to cross God. To wish my sister misery because she had chased me down for borrowing her socks, to feel resentful toward my mother for forcing me to do chores when I'd rather be playing with the neighborhood friends, were thoughts that burdened me with guilt. But here, in the pages of my first book about Judaism, I found a more loving, compassionate God, one that humanized us. In Judaism I could think whatever I wanted to. In fact, it was expected of me. The fact that I didn't act on my every thought was what mattered.

Kushner explained that Jews believe God creates nothing that is vile or useless. Food, sex, sleep — all can be made holy and sacred. I read that sin is a deed, not a condition. After years of hearing, "We are all sinners!" it was refreshing to learn that people are thought to be both good and bad. In fact, the two conflicting tendencies are a natural state. It is simply our job to monitor them. In Judaism, a sin is a not an offense against *God*. It is a missed opportunity to act humanely, seen as "missing the target."

The Jewish way of repenting was particularly appealing to me. Jews believe that God gave us the power to repent. This is a form of regret and change as a result of what we have come to understand. Repentance is not complete until we come into the same situation and act differently. This seemed such common sense! Again, simply asking God for forgiveness is not the key. The key is in behaving differently the next time. Night after night, after putting Harrison to bed, I read *To Life!* and became increasingly excited by the tenets by which I could live my life. I could foresee actually forgiving myself for not being perfect. Kushner wrote about embracing our errors. I had always believed we were placed on this earth to learn and grow, yet the Catholicism I was raised in put little emphasis on the lesson, focusing instead on the mistake. In Judaism, we are *supposed* to make mistakes, for only by our errors can we learn. Some Jews believe that human beings are actually on a higher moral plane than angels. Angels never do anything wrong. Human beings do plenty of things wrong but have the capacity to learn from mistakes and grow.

As I wrote down all of the ideas in Judaism that thrilled me, I also made asterisks alongside burning questions. If Jews are the chosen people, what does that make the rest of us? What is the Jewish philosophy on life after death? Why do Jews see death as a tragedy? What is the significance of keeping kosher in a home?

I returned to Rabbi Sirkman's office nearly one month after our first visit. Again I was welcomed with a hearty hello, the greeting of a dear friend.

"So, what did you think of the book?"

"Rabbi…I don't know where to begin. It's just that, well, it all makes sense! I had no idea Judaism would fit me so well."

"Tell me!"

As I flipped through my notebook, reciting Harold Kushner's passages as if revealing ideas to a beginning student, the rabbi listened attentively, as if hearing the words for the first time. I stopped at a few questions.

"I'm having a hard time with the idea that the Jews perceive themselves as the chosen people. Does that mean I'm not chosen, nor is my family? Do Jews consider us inferior to them in God's eyes?"

The rabbi described what was written in the Torah, that the Jews were chosen to pass along God's message. "That's what's written in the Torah. But I believe that each and every one of us chooses to be chosen."

I looked at him and understood. We can live our lives, appreciating our gifts, giving back to others, reveling in the joys of life, or we cannot. We choose.

"I have another question."

"Go on!" I felt that he was genuinely excited by the questions I posed, not knowing what I would ask next. I paused for a moment, thinking how I could *never* have felt comfortable asking a priest such pointed questions. It would have seemed entirely disrespectful.

"Death."

"Yes."

"What do Jews believe?"

"In Reform Judaism, we know what we don't know. We don't know what happens after death. We may like to think there is life after death, and some believe in reincarnation. But one thing we do know: dead is dead. So we live our lives to the fullest, not for the reward of the afterlife, but for the reward of life."

This was thrilling; life itself *was* magical to me. I, myself, wavered between believing in reincarnation and not knowing what to believe at all.

"Do Jews believe in heaven?"

"We don't know if there is a heaven. So we do all we can to make heaven right here on earth."

In Reform Judaism, what I believed about life after death wasn't important. How I lived my life was. Suddenly, it all gelled. The Jewish weddings with an abundance of food and dancing, the Jewish way of doing charity work and contributing to the world... all were part of living life fully.

My heart leapt with anticipation as I went through the rest of my questions. How could I learn more? Could it possibly get any better?

Before I could ask Rabbi Sirkman what my next step was, he offered me another book: *God Was Not in the Fire*, by Daniel

Gordis. I graciously tried to decline his offer, wanting instead to buy my own copy to write notes in, but he insisted I take the book from his shelf, telling me it was an extra from the temple book club. I clutched the soft cover against my chest as I departed. I could hardly wait until Harrison's bedtime.

Choosing

The trees of our quiet suburb stood stoic and spindly, their barren branches exposed to the wind and snow. I was amazed at how quickly the summer rolled into autumn, autumn surrendering to the early days of winter.

I had been studying with Rabbi Sirkman for six months, reading books that answered many of my questions about Judaism and enlightened me about new concepts as well. I finally accepted that my Jewish friends could feel their religion was important to them even without their understanding the major beliefs about their faith. In *God Was Not in the Fire* Daniel Gordis suggested that people refuse to let go of Jewish life, not because it has been incredibly gratifying, but because they deeply suspect it has more to offer. I wondered if this was true of Michael's friends and family. Were they grasping at some value in their religion that was just beyond their reach? Did they keep their fingers on the surface of Judaism in hopes of feeling the surging power beneath the veneer?

The significance of the Torah became clearer, too. Since first stepping into Central Synagogue, I had wondered what was so important about the Torah for the Jews. While in Catholicism there was great respect for the Bible as the guidepost for life, in Judaism the Torah was absolutely revered. This was first evident for me during High Holy Day services. The rabbi removed the Torah from the ark and held it high above his head for all to see. He then cradled it in his arms and walked up and down the aisles of the synagogue as people reached out to touch the covered Torah with their prayer books, then touched the books to their lips. Only when the parade was complete were the scrolls uncovered — the fitted cloth and the band securing it removed — and the Torah set down on the podium. To read from the Torah is considered a great honor. In fact, one cannot read from the Torah until the age of 13, when one is considered an adult in Judaism. It was so different from what I was accustomed to. At Our Lady of Lourdes, the priest approached the pulpit, opened the Holy Bible and read.

While all the pomp highlighted the great respect for the Torah, I had been unclear as to why. Was I to consider the Torah a compilation of factual stories, a recording of history? Did Jews think God wrote every word? Even as a young girl listening to readings in church, I questioned the odds of the Bible stories having been recorded accurately. Did Judaism suggest that we take the stories at face value? Gordis succeeded in helping me find my own value in the Torah. He proposed that the Torah be considered the journal of the Jewish people. Imagine if I had hunted around my attic and come across an aged diary of my great-great-great-grandparent. Wouldn't I fervently search for traces of myself in the faded pages? The Torah is just that — stories of ancestors in which we could find vestiges of ourselves. Did I carry the traits of Moses, a reluctant leader? Or perhaps I had the kindness and protectiveness of Miriam, Moses' sister, who watched out for him as the river carried him downstream in a basket. The possibilities of learning more about myself through the Torah stories enticed me.

There were ancient Jewish traditions that I didn't understand, including the practice of keeping kosher. I had no exposure to a kosher home, with the exception of my neighbors in Larchmont. While they explained that keeping kosher meant a diet without shellfish and pork, that meat and dairy must not be eaten from the same plate and utensils, and that all food must have kosher certification, the importance of this tradition remained unclear. I knew that eating kosher reflected dietary laws that had survived thousands of years, reflecting environmental restrictions from biblical times, but what was the significance of keeping kosher in contemporary times? Was it simply to continue an ancient tradition? Most of the Jewish people I knew would never consider keeping kosher, for the same reason it hadn't occurred to me — I did not perceive any value in it.

In my studies, *Renewing the Covenant* offered the first explanation that made sense to me. Eugene Borowitz described traditions, such as keeping kosher, as a way to increase the odds for spiritual moments. We spend our lives in habitual routines punctuated by moments of inspiration. Judaism suggests that we don't have to wait for a sky streaked in the vibrant colors of sunset or the sound of a child's unfettered laughter to experience a rush of joy or moment of meaning. Perhaps lighting the Sabbath candles will remind a mother of her own childhood, and the memory of her father's smile will warm her. In that moment of light, she may experience the security in the flow of life. Packing boxes of clothing for a charitable cause may create a sense of compassion and gratitude. And keeping kosher, eating mindfully at every meal, may make sacred an otherwise everyday action. Judaism compiled a list of 613 *mitzvot*, laws to observe in day-to-day life. We cannot predict how these rites may enlighten us. There are no guarantees there will be any sort of spiritual shift at all. But by merely opening the door to let God into routine moments, the odds that God will walk through dramatically increase.

I was surprised how embracing Judaism had been more daunting in theory than in action. For all the angst I had experienced in my search for a religion, studying Judaism was almost effortless. Before reading *To Life!*, I held the conviction that I would not remotely consider converting unless Judaism became important to me personally. My test was simple: if for any reason

Michael and I were no longer together, would I be glad for my new faith? Until studying, reading and talking about Judaism, I couldn't imagine feeling that way. Yet, as I found that its philosophies were a reflection of my existing beliefs, I felt as if I was already Jewish. It was my childhood blanket reappearing after years of absence, billowing from the sky, dropping onto my body and molding itself to my form. Judaism gave me a comfort and meaningfulness I hadn't felt in years, perhaps ever. The more I read about and discussed my studies, the more I felt I was reentering familiar territory. It was like coming home.

Sometime in the first two months of my studies, I sat down in the rabbi's office and announced that I wanted to convert to Judaism.

"That's wonderful," he smiled and nodded knowingly.

"I'm really happy." A sense of relief and elation flooded me. I had found my religion, and the anticipation of learning more about it created the sort of giddiness of having a crush. "Do I need to take a class?"

"Well, the class at the Jewish Community Center of Westchester started already. The next session isn't for another year—"

I was deflated. Would I have to wait a full year? Or would I instead commute into Manhattan to take a class? I crossed my legs tightly and intertwined my fingers as two impossible choices wrestled in my mind — enrolling in another course at the dreaded 92nd Street Y or slowing my momentum and postponing my studies.

"— and by then you'll be way ahead of their material. You and I will study together. It will be great!"

A more enormous gift I couldn't imagine. The thought of studying one-on-one with the most inspiring teacher I had ever known, overwhelmed me.

"That's wonderful," I squeaked through my choked-up throat.

"So, let's begin!"

"Wai t— when does the actual conversion take place?"

"We won't set a date."

"We won't?"

"No. No date." the rabbi leaned forward, reaching for his notebook.

"I mean — will it take six months? A year?"

"Who knows?" He threw his hands up.

I was not in the mood for riddles. I wanted to know what to expect. Should I envision my official conversion in the spring, as new leaves start to fill out the bare branches and our new baby is a few months old? Would it be scheduled around my birthday the following autumn, a double celebration at our house for our friends and family?

"You'll know when you're ready."

"I will?"

"You will."

***

That December, my readings and meetings were interrupted for a few months for the most glorious reason — the birth of Olivia. Yet amidst the flurry of activity around the birth of a child, I found my mindset had already become Jewish.

Judaism places huge emphasis on the naming of children, believing that the name of a person is closely related to the child's fundamental qualities. When a parent gives a child a name, a connection is created between the baby and previous generations. With the baby's name, the parents are also making a statement about their hope for who their child will become. The naming in honor of a late relative, usually done by using the initial of the first name of the deceased, carries with it some identity for the son or daughter.

We wanted to name our baby after Michael's late brother, Anthony. As one "A" option after another dropped out for various reasons, we struggled with a list of names we didn't love. Yet Michael and I were equally passionate that Tony be honored in our child's name. Finally, moments after our daughter was born, we chose Olivia.

"But we have to name her after your brother!" I found myself stating emphatically. "It's so important!" In Olivia I saw not only our newborn daughter, but a child with a heritage, a history she knew nothing about yet. I wanted her name to remind her of who she is, and who came before her.

"Ann," Michael reassured me. "Let's have her middle name be the memory of my brother."

Soon after Olivia's birth, I planned my first Jewish rite of passage — the baby naming. Just two-and-a-half years earlier, I had vehemently opposed the mere suggestion that we have a *bris* for newborn Harrison. In no way had I wanted my child to be circumcised in our house. "I will not have my child's penis cut, then all break for bagels," I had stated firmly. Nor did I understand the need for a Hebrew name, a custom I thought would make me feel alien to my children and husband. Now, with Olivia's birth, I was not only willing to invite friends and family into our living room, which was temporarily furnished with wicker furniture and folding chairs; I wanted to have the people I love welcome our daughter into the world, granting her a Hebrew name in a room of Jewish people, proclaiming her name as an honor to her late uncle.

***

One wintry day, while sitting in Rabbi Sirkman's office discussing the latest book I had read, the rabbi startled me with a request.

"February 9th is our Outreach Service."

"Outreach?"

"It's the service dedicated to reaching out to those in the community who may not feel connected."

The rabbi went on to explain that the Outreach Committee was dedicated to meeting the needs of interfaith families. I was amazed such a group existed, considering years ago I had heard two rabbis decry interfaith marriages. Larchmont Temple outreach, including one Sabbath dinner and service each year, not only provided opportunities to learn more about Judaism, but also to meet other members of the temple, including interfaith families.

"That sounds nice. Do you think I should go?"

"I think you should speak."

"Speak? At the service? What would I say?" I couldn't fathom what I could offer an interfaith group. I knew so little about Judaism. I was in the early stages of my education.

"Talk about your journey!" The rabbi smiled and threw his hands forward, as if it would be the most natural thing in the world to do.

"My journey?"

"Sure! Tell us why you're here. Why you're converting."

I considered this idea. While I did like to talk to my friends about my conversion, I just didn't see why a roomful of interfaith couples and Jews would be interested in my story.

"But why me?"

"You have a great story to tell!"

"I do?" I was genuinely perplexed. I was just a woman converting to Judaism. How interesting could that be? Yet if the rabbi wanted me to speak, I would continue my lifelong habit of trying to please people, particularly teachers, and acquiesce.

"How long does my talk have to be?"

"Five minutes. Eight. Whatever comes naturally to you."

Five to eight minutes, I thought. I was accustomed to giving 45-minute presentations for work, so the time requirement was a relief. It was the notion of collecting my thoughts about my conversion that overwhelmed me. How could I synopsize my journey? I couldn't even pinpoint the beginning. Did it start with my meeting with Rabbi Sirkman? Or did my journey start as a teenager, when I decided not to get confirmed in the Catholic Church? How could I possibly describe the indescribable, that Judaism seemed always to be my religion?

Two weeks later Michael and I stepped into the temple sanctuary for the Sabbath service. The last time I was here, during the High Holy Days, the hundreds of people crowding the sanctuary overpowered me. I hadn't noticed that the Larchmont Temple sanctuary had an uncanny resemblance to Our Lady of Lourdes. Oak pews parted to form a center aisle leading to a low platform. A podium stood at the front edge of the bema, with two slender microphones mounted to each corner and bent into graceful elbows.

I surveyed our options for seating. Knowing I would be speaking halfway through the service, I felt it would be appropriate to sit up front in the first few pews. Yet that felt too conspicuous. On some level, I wanted to hide and blend into the crowd. Michael and I slid into aisle seats in the middle of the sanctuary. I was struck by how there couldn't have been more than 150 people in attendance. It seemed sparse in contrast to Rosh Hashanah and Yom Kippur.

"Are you nervous?" Michael whispered to the side of my head.

I fixed my eyes on the bema and smiled.

"Absolutely."

"How will you know when to speak?"

"I guess the rabbi will let me know."

I opened my purse for the third time that evening, making sure my three typed and folded pages were there.

As the rabbinic procession began, I surveyed my surroundings. The pale beige walls, interrupted by contemporary stained-glass windows along one side, were unadorned except for the dozen or so quilted banners hanging against them. I suddenly remembered a detail of Our Lady of Lourdes — felt banners suspended from gold dowels depicting various Psalms quotes.

The banners in Larchmont Temple's sanctuary were written in Hebrew, and I wondered what they said.

Having never attended a Friday night service up to this point, I had no idea when one speaks from the bema. The rabbi had told me it would be about halfway through the service. But when would that be? Was this an hour service? What if it were two — or more, like Rosh Hashanah and Yom Kippur? In addition to my concern about timing, I suddenly wondered if the words I had prepared were at all appropriate. I had a habit of being direct and candid when speaking to friends or writing late at night, which was precisely when I had written my talk. Had I overstepped any boundaries? Was it possible my speech was too honest and revealing about my journey? I quickly reassured myself that Michael had liked it, remembering how he came into the bedroom with tears in his eyes, having stumbled upon it on the desk in the den, telling me what I had written was beautiful. But he was my husband... would it make sense to strangers?

That Michael now sat next to me during Friday night services was profoundly touching. In my last few months of studying Judaism, it seemed that the more excited I was, the more withdrawn Michael became.

"Ooh, Michael! Listen to this!" I would exclaim, wanting to share an author's ideas that I thought he would relate to. Michael would politely listen, then nod, saying, "That's nice," then go back to whatever he was doing.

Once, after reading *The Sabbath* by Abraham Joshua Heschel, I told Michael I would be interested in observing the Sabbath every Friday.

"What? Like walk everywhere and not spend money on Saturday?" I knew from my readings that Michael was referring to the Orthodox Jewish manner of observing the Sabbath. Work of any kind is prohibited from sundown Friday to sundown Saturday. In addition to work of the conventional type, such as jobs and lawn chores, it also includes driving a car, turning on a light switch and more, since those actions require moving objects and igniting fuel. What Michael didn't consider was that the Sabbath is about play, rest and relaxation. The laws of Judaism encourage people to take a stroll, sing, attend lectures, read, and make love. It is a time to gather with friends and family without distractions and superficialities like shopping, errands and obligations. Yet by Michael's furrowed brow and his tone that implied I'd suggested something preposterous, I knew better than to explain the rewards of observing the 24-hour Sabbath.

"I meant having the Sabbath dinner."

"The Sabbath dinner? Next you're going to want to keep kosher!"

I sighed, deciding to postpone the conversation, hoping he might come around in time. I was beginning to understand the significance of Jewish customs and, while I didn't foresee having the discipline for most of the practices, I certainly respected them. It frustrated me that Michael seemed unnerved by my enthusiasm and by Judaism in general. I found myself daydreaming about how nice it would be to be married to someone who might try to refrain from shopping for just one Saturday, exploring whether it had any impact on our family.

At the very least, I had hoped Michael would show some interest in what I was learning about his religion. Instead, I realized that Michael didn't want to learn any more than he already knew and that he was defensive about any suggestion of observance beyond attending temple for the High Holy Days. It was simply "too Jewish." My earnestness was a lot for him, and I reminded myself that Judaism was my spiritual journey, not his.

It wasn't until Michael read the three pages he found on the desk that he showed any level of interest or attention at all. By his mere attendance tonight, I didn't assume or hope his devotion to Judaism would deepen. I was simply glad that, for the moment, my husband supported me.

I tried to follow the Gates of Prayer with the page-number

prompts Rabbi Sirkman periodically announced. The prayer book interspersed Hebrew, the transliteration of the Hebrew, and English, offering non-Hebrew-speaking congregants the chance to follow along.

"L'chah do-di lik-rat ka-lah, p'nei Shabbat n'ka-b'lah. Beloved, come to meet the bride; beloved, come to greet the Shabbat."

My focused attempt to follow the text distracted me from my rising agitation, so when the rabbi announced my name, I was momentarily caught unaware.

"… Sally Friedes, a student of conversion.…" Michael patted my thigh and told me I would do great as I stood up from the pew.

My heels clicked on the marble floor as I walked down the long aisle, a stretch of floor that seemed to lengthen with each step. I hoped the people I passed couldn't see the rubber band that fastened my skirt under my suit jacket, a trick I'd learned from other mothers who had to wear pre-maternity suits after giving birth. Before I could reach the rabbi to greet him, he smiled, sat down in the front pew, and motioned me to the bema.

I took my place behind the broad wood pedestal, unfolded my papers and examined the faces in the sanctuary — senior citizens and middle-aged couples gazing at me expectantly. I smiled and glanced down at my notes.

"Friends and family have asked me how or why I decided to convert to Judaism. The answer is never a simple one. It's not as easy as 'my husband is Jewish' or 'I want our kids to be Jewish.' "

I described Michael's marriage proposal and my initial desire years ago to educate myself in Judaism, and I recounted my roadblocks, including the 92nd Street Y and my first Central Synagogue sermon. I looked out at the clusters of congregants, was struck by their attentiveness, and continued.

"I opened up countless conversations with Jewish friends and family about their identities as Jews. This led to only more confusion. I didn't meet one Jewish person who knew anything about their religion! How could their faith be so important to them when they didn't know the meaning behind their traditions and holidays? When they didn't know what any particular Hebrew prayer meant? I was appalled to learn that many Jewish people didn't even know if they believed in God! This certainly wasn't the religion for me. What did Jews believe in? No one knew."

As I alternately read from my typed pages and looked out into the crowd, I wondered if I had startled the congregation with my candor. Worse yet, had I insulted anyone by criticizing their lack of knowledge about their faith? I thought back to Our Lady of Lourdes, how in all my years of attending services there Sunday after Sunday for 13 years, I had never seen anyone stand at the altar questioning Catholicism. Had I offended this audience with the description of the exclusion and hypocrisy I had experienced over the years?

"That same year, I attended temple for the High Holy Days. I felt as if the rabbi were talking directly to me. He explained that there is Judaism the heritage and Judaism the religion. And both are valid reasons for being Jewish." My words bundled in my throat as I remembered the moment I had heard the rabbi's talk that opened the door to my new faith.

"And it became clear to me, it was all right that I would not be part of the heritage. My ancestors were not Jewish. But I can certainly embrace Judaism as a religion. Which was exactly what I was looking for."

As one word flowed to the next, my story started to make sense to me. No longer did my path to Judaism seem a puzzle of random experiences. I had connected the dots. Describing how life had become so much fuller since studying Judaism, the truth of the statement resonated with me.

"… I have the best of everything. I get to learn about a religion I have chosen. My husband gets to learn about a heritage he was born into. And our children will understand and live the meaningfulness of both." I paused and looked into a congregation that had given me their undivided attention.

"When I think about my journey into Judaism, a very specific image comes to mind. I am walking through an ancient stone archway into the most beautiful, luscious garden I have ever seen. Birds are singing and flying overhead, the scents are magnificent, and I'm carrying with me my own flowers, unique in their own way."

I took my eyes away from the pages, looking into the faces of the gray-haired couples and the younger professionals, and I spoke from memory.

"What strikes me is there are no gates in this garden. All are welcome to enter and enjoy, experience and contribute. And that is exactly what I am doing."

Retracing my steps to my seat, I was taken by the warm smiles and nods. The moment I sat down, a balding man in front of me turned and said, with a tear in his eye, "No one has spoken exactly how I've always felt. That was wonderful."

I took in his kindly look, the peace in his eyes. I had expected to tell my personal story. I hadn't foreseen it reflecting the lives of those sitting before me.

"That was great, honey. You did great." Michael beamed.

I turned my attention back to Rabbi Sirkman as he stepped onto the bema and opened his prayer book. He glanced up, smiled and closed his book, throwing his hands in the air. The motion, signaling *What else is there to say?* evoked a burst of laughter from the congregation. I looked down at my hands folded in my lap and blushed. I hardly felt worthy of this high praise.

The rest of the service, the Torah portion, the reciting of the mourner's prayers and the temple announcements, flew by in what seemed to be minutes. After the rabbi walked to the back of the sanctuary, ending the service, I expected to sneak out the side door with Michael. Not knowing anyone made me feel uncomfortable, and I was ready to go home. Instead, men and women surrounded me, patting my back, complimenting me on my talk.

"You described exactly the conundrum I've always felt: How can I not believe in God, yet have Judaism be important to me?"

"I've been so guilty of that — not knowing anything about my religion. But I would never consider abandoning Judaism."

"My daughter-in-law converted to Judaism, too. You should talk to her."

Caught in the flow of people going to the anteroom to have *challah* and wine, I found myself next to a small, elderly woman with rounded shoulders and short, fluffy white curls. Wrinkles splayed in sunburst lines around her eyes, a piercing blue behind her wire-rimmed glasses.

"Darling. Your talk was wonderful. My name is Rosel."

Her heavy European accent and gravelly voice beguiled me; I wondered what stories she could tell, what life she had led.

"If you want to learn Hebrew, come and see me. I teach Hebrew to all the conversion students."

"Hebrew?"

"Yes, darling. Hebrew. It'll be good for you to learn it for the *Shema*."

Shema? Hebrew? I thought I was just reading books.

"Ask the rabbi. He'll give you my number." She squeezed my forearm as if the decision had been made and it was just a matter of logistics. As she walked off to the center of the crowd, taking with her a faint scent of lavender, I remained motionless for a moment, completely perplexed. No one — and by no one I meant the rabbi — had mentioned learning Hebrew. I had never learned a foreign language in my life. Now, learning a new alphabet and language? I knew I had better follow this up with Rabbi Sirkman.

"Michael. Did you hear her name??"

"Rosel? I think it was Rosel."

I looked off into the crowd, now moving toward the challah table.

"Do you think I can learn Hebrew?"

Michael grinned, shaking his head. "I think you can do just about anything you want."

Learning Jewish

I felt jarred out of my environment when I found myself leaving Larchmont to drive to my first Hebrew lesson in Mamaroneck, just a few miles from our home. A long lane of mid-century houses divided by a wide, grassy meridian distinguished this area as quintessential suburbia, a bedroom community to Manhattan. The sterile row of homes felt very different from my neighborhood. In Larchmont, corner parks dotted winding lanes, and hilly roads of eclectic houses made for interesting meandering. I walked with friends to the playground and passed other mothers with strollers. They reminded me that I was surrounded by likeminded families who had traded in the über-metropolitan lifestyle of New York for award-winning schools and a slower paced life.

As I neared Rosel's home, less than one block from the Long Island Sound, it struck me that I had no sense of being near the water. It was starkly different from the Manor, the shoreline neighborhood in Larchmont of palatial, shingled, turn-of-the-century Victorian "cottages" and stucco Mediterranean mansions. It was in the Manor that I could feel the essence of Larchmont's history as a summer community for the Manhattan elite. I often claimed an hour or two of solitude in the Manor Park early on weekend mornings, walking the winding paths and sitting on the rugged rocks along the water's edge to write in my journal. Taking in the moist sea air and watching other people on their leisurely strolls, it was easy to imagine women in petticoats and parasols and gentlemen in top hats ambling along the very same paths. There was no salty breeze near Rosel's house nor the clanging of bells from moored boats to draw me in. I could have been in any suburb in any town in the country.

Pulling into Rosel's driveway, I parked my car alongside the tiered fountain that gurgled in front of the split-level house and sat in my car for a moment. The night of the Outreach Service had turned out to be a pivotal point in my conversion. In that short span of two hours, I was yanked from the solitude of my studies, inserted into a Jewish congregation, and confronted with the information that learning Hebrew was to be part of my conversion studies.

Until this moment, studying Judaism had been a pleasantly reclusive experience. I read my books at home, discussed them with the rabbi during our meetings, and read some more. With the exception of anonymously attending a service or two, I had no interaction with anyone in the temple except for greeting the administrative staff as I passed by their desks. Did I want to leave my shelter and enter the unknown and intimidating temple culture? Would the spell be broken when I ventured outside of my comfort zone? Would people accept me as a student of Judaism, or would they consider me a woman who had stepped outside her domain?

And a foreign language! Inexplicably, I had skated through high school and college, including studying overseas, without one single foreign language course. Now, not only would I need to learn another language, I would have to master a completely new alphabet.

Days after the Outreach Service, when I had spoken with the rabbi, I entered the conversation wondering if I needed to learn Hebrew at all. Of the Jewish friends and family I knew, only a handful could fumble through passages written in Hebrew, and fewer yet understood what they were reading, having little or no Hebrew vocabulary. Most of Michael's friends had learned only what they needed to know to get through their bar or bat mitzvahs and never gave the language a second thought after that. If most people who were born into Judaism had no understanding of Hebrew, then why was I, as a convert, required to surpass their standards?

I approached the conversation with the rabbi tentatively. "I met Rosel at the Outreach Service, and she mentioned that she teaches Hebrew ..."

"Excellent! This is a great time to start Hebrew lessons." The rabbi responded with his trademark enthusiasm.

Still unclear whether Hebrew was a requirement, I delved further. "Is this something every conversion student does? I mean, is there a deadline — will I have to read or speak Hebrew on the day I convert?" If I didn't need the language for the actual act of converting, I might be able to construct a case to indefinitely delay my lessons altogether.

"Absolutely. You'll be reading the Shema at your conversion," he said offhandedly, as if I knew what the "shma" was.

"The Shema?"

"Yes. It's one of the basic Jewish prayers, declaring your faith in God. It's also an affirmation of being Jewish. You'll need to recite it in Hebrew."

Reciting a prayer in Hebrew? The thought was unfathomable. A familiar tension clenched my stomach. "Won't it take a long time to learn Hebrew?"

"You'll do fine. Ask Cynthia for Rosel's phone number and you can get started right away."

Sitting in my car now, trepidation clouding my thoughts, I forced myself to remember the potential payoffs of learning Hebrew. It would be wonderful to read the Passover Haggadah as well as the posters that hung in the temple corridors. I entertained the possibility of understanding the songs we sang in temple and of reading the prayer book. I imagined understanding the Hebrew blessings when I lit the menorah at Hanukkah, teaching them to my children. With my intentions realigned, I unclasped Olivia's car seat, hoisted her up, walked to the front door and rang the doorbell.

"Come in, dear! The door is open!"

I entered a dim space that looked like a throwback to the recreation rooms of my childhood. The paneled walls, darkening a space that already begged for natural light, enveloped a room with a wet bar, a sagging sofa and a weathered coffee table. The light from the sliding glass doors illuminated stacks of boxes and a pile of clothing on hangers draped over the bar. Before I could further absorb my surroundings, Rosel peeked over the railing of the open staircase, dabbing her short curls with a towel.

"I just finished a swim. Ignore the mess down there — I'm getting things together for a woman's shelter. Come up, dear."

I climbed the carpeted stairs and entered a sun-drenched expanse of a room. The mid-century furniture looked unworn and immaculate, the cushions on the long, narrow sofa firm and the wooden tables unblemished. The cool sleekness of the room was warmed by stacks of books on the oversized coffee table and countless framed photographs and books lining the built-in shelves.

"Is the baby all right?"

I looked down at Olivia sleeping soundly in her car seat.

"For the moment. I have her bottle if she wakes up."

"She's adorable. So sweet. Come. Sit down. Do you want something to drink?

I had been nervous when I called Rosel, but when I heard her cheery accent over the phone, a peculiar twinge of affinity overcame me, a sensation that put me at ease. Hearing Rosel in her living room now, I pinpointed the source of my nostalgia. I was transported back to the kitchen of my great-aunt Nina, my father's Yugoslavian aunt in Milwaukee. Visiting her and Uncle Tony in their modest bungalow on the Southside meant endless pans of warm strudel and glasses of cold milk, and big-bosomed hugs in Aunt Nina's welcoming arms. There must have been something very special in the strudel, because by the time I left Aunt Nina's kitchenette, I felt satiated on every level— fed, nurtured and loved unconditionally.

"Those are for you, dear." Rosel ushered me to a large 1950s dining table, empty except for a stack of loose-leaf papers. She noticed me eyeing them apprehensively.

"We'll get to those in a second, dear. But, first, tell me, how far along are you in your conversion?"

"I've been studying with the rabbi for about a year."

"That's good! Jeffrey is wonderful. What made you want to convert?"

As I reached down and tucked Olivia's blanket around her compact body, I summoned my thoughts about my story. I wasn't sure how to explain how I fell in love with the values of Judaism and how the culture enraptured me.

"Well, I was raised Catholic, but I really haven't observed Catholicism for a long time. So I started looking for other religions."

"But your husband, is he Jewish?"

"Well, yes, he was raised Reform. But he's not the reason I'm converting. Judaism has really come to mean something to *me*."

"That's good! I'm sure he and his family are happy you're converting."

"Well, yes, my mother-in-law is thrilled. Just the other day she introduced me to a friend, saying, 'This is my daughter-in-law. She's converting to Judaism, you know.'"

Rosel laughed and as we continued talking, I became as comfortable as if I were sitting at my Aunt Nina's table. When she reached over and patted my hand, I took in her knuckles, bulky with age, and thought how good it felt to be around someone older and wiser than myself. As a child, I hadn't spent much time with my grandparents. My father's parents died when I was young, and my mother's parents lived several hours away. When we did see each other, the children were discharged to other rooms so the adults could visit exclusively. Throughout my life, I wondered what it would have been like to have a wise senior to turn to for advice. There were so many questions that their years of wisdom could have answered — how important is my choice of college major? Should I stay home and raise the kids or go back to work? How can I navigate through the tough times in marriage? I sometimes yearned for a sense of perspective my youth couldn't offer. Although I greatly valued my parents' opinions, talking with my friends' grandparents and elderly neighbors was always comforting, too. Their perspective came from a lifetime of romances, births, deaths, careers, accidents, heartbreaks and losses. People of an older generation seemed to have a sense of how all the pieces fit together to create a mosaic of life, an outlook that I found magnetizing.

Over the last few years, I had come to appreciate Bernice's complex experiences. During our times having lunch together in the city or swimming alone in the Hamptons, my mother-in-law slowly revealed the painful layers of her life that her exterior smile concealed. She told me of a trying childhood with a terminally ill mother and an emotionally volatile father, a man who was later diagnosed with bipolar disorder. She relived the night her late son, Tony, died, and found it nearly impossible to mention his name without experiencing his death all over again. Not a day went by when she did not miss him. She confessed a difficult relationship between an adolescent Michael and his father, revealing a hypercritical parent whom my husband rarely spoke of, but with whom he later became close. I heard of Bernice's college days as a beautiful co-ed with three different dates a day, about her life as a vibrant stage actress in New York, and later, as a fashionable Upper East Side mother who doted on her children. I loved and respected her more and more with each story. When Bernice entered our Larchmont house every weekend, her "Hello, everyone!" booming in our hallway, her soft hands cupping my face for a kiss on the cheek, I felt the love of a wise woman who accepted her hardships and lived fully the blessings of her life.

Sitting in Mamaroneck, I found that same level of contentment in Rosel's eyes, a deep calmness I was certain came from accepting the myriad of life's experiences. Smiles came easily to Rosel, and as she listened to me intently, my confidence was bolstered. How hard could it be to learn Hebrew? People all over the world studied languages that were not native to them — I could do this.

"Okay, dear. Let's take a look at the first page."

I flipped over the first paper and stopped. In front of me was a chart of 40 symbols that looked ludicrously similar to one another.

"Don't worry about that page" She tapped the paper. "That will be your reference. Go to the next page."

She took note of my startled look.

"Don't look there, either. Too soon."

She turned the third page for me.

"Or that one." Nothing I had glimpsed on any of the papers looked remotely familiar, and I was starting to get nervous.

"Perfect!" Rosel tapped a printout with two oversized letters at the top of the page, and miniature versions of them below. "Let's start here."

I stared at what looked like a backward, angular *c* sitting atop a short horizontal line beneath it. The open side of the 'c' encompassed a polka dot.

"This is a letter, right?"

"That is a *bet*. The sound is like *buh*."

"Buh," I repeated, as if I had a bad taste on my lips I was trying to spit out.

"Yes, *buh*. The symbol below it is the vowel."

I leaned forward and noticed the miniature capital *T* below the *bet*.

"It has the 'ah' sound. Go ahead, dear. Try it."

I eyed the combination suspiciously.

"I'll say it first," Rosel jumped in. "Bah."

"Bah."

"Very good!" Rosel exclaimed with the exuberance of a parent praising a child's crayon scrawl . And I appreciated it. "Now, try these words below."

"Bah bah. Bah bah. Bah. Bah."

"Wonderful. See? It's not so hard. Now, this next letter is a *vet*."

"No, it's not," I pointed out. "That's the *bet* again."

"No, dear. It's a *vet*."

"But it looks like a *bet*."

"There is no dot in the *vet*."

"Are you kidding me? I've got to look for dots to tell the difference between two letters?" I knew the *bet* had been too easy.

Rosel laughed. "Go ahead. Try it."

I sighed. "Vah. Vah vah. Vahvah. Vah…Vahbah."

"Excellent! See? You're getting it!"

"What do these words mean?"

"Oh, they're gibberish. They don't mean anything. They're just to get you used to the sounds."

Olivia stirred and wailed her hungry cry.

"This is a good place to stop, Sally. Now, let's see that baby. Who knows? Maybe she'll learn Hebrew with you!"

***

Week after week, I climbed the stairs to the serene environment of Rosel's living room, with the far-reaching goal of learning a very difficult language. My progress was slow. Each lesson I was confronted by squiggly, angular symbols that made me feel like a tourist visiting a foreign land. Each day was a new adventure in the Hebrew alphabet.

One day I turned the page to see a figure that looked like a house with a domed roof, a puff of smoke coming out of a chimney on the left. It sat atop a flat line with a gap on the left side, creating an open doorway.

"This is a *mem*," Rosel said. "It sounds like an *m*."

"And what is that letter next to it?" I pointed to an upright rectangle with a cowlick on the side.

"That is the final *mem*."

"Final *mem*?"

"Yes, dear. That is what the *mem* looks like at the end of the word."

"But it doesn't look anything like the *mem*."

"That's because it's not a *mem*. It is a *final mem*."

"Why can't there just be one *mem*?" I knew there was no logic in expressing my exasperation to Rosel. It was not as if she had the power to alter the Hebrew alphabet. I just needed to lodge my complaint somewhere.

"Dear, there are a few final letters. Take a look at the *final nun*," she flipped the page to a tall, elongated line with a glop of ink for the head. "This looks a little different from the *nun*, which is much smaller." I peered at the *nun*, a small square sliced vertically in half. I saw no relation between it and the *final nun* at all.

On the other hand, unrelated letters looked almost identical. The *pay* looked like a backward *bet*, the *fay* looked like *pay*, which also resembled the final *nun*. I felt like a child examining two seemingly matching drawings in a game book, trying to determine what minuscule variation made them different. When I was introduced to the *kaf*, I wondered why I was learning the *bet* all over again.

"No, dear," Rosel said. See the bottom line of the *bet*? There is a little notch in it."

I put my nose closer to the paper and squinted.

"A notch?"

"See? The *kaf* is curved. No notch. That's how you know it is a *kaf*."

The rules of pronunciation were like none in the English

language. I read confounding instructions such as "This is the vowel *shvah*. This vowel has no sound." Strangely, this vowel showed up in the middle of words for no apparent reason. Why have the vowel at all?

The more I studied Hebrew, the more empathy I had for Harrison as he learned to read in kindergarten. I understood how overwhelming it was to look at an array of symbols and attempt to transform them into words. Yet I also envied him. If he read aloud and mispronounced a word, he would know it, hearing a sound that made no sense. In my Hebrew lessons, I had no such reality check. Now and then Rosel would point out that I had inadvertently pronounced an actual word and I would be delighted, jotting the English translation in the margin of the page. But more typically, I was reciting nonsense. When I studied at home, with no transliterations to check my pronunciations against and no vocabulary to use as a reality check, I had no idea whether I was making mistakes or not.

Progress was tediously slow, but as the months passed, I was starting to make headway. I was able to recognize the letters from the beginning of the alphabet, and word recognition started to register. When I could read *ima*, the translation for "mother," and *abba*, Hebrew for "father," as an entire word, rather than a letter-by-letter pronunciation, I started to get a taste of what it would be like to actually read and understand the original language of Judaism. *Teacher*, *house*, and *Torah*, soon followed. I was starting to feel confident in my potential — until Rosel announced it was time to study the Shema. After fumbling over the words of the 20-line prayer repeatedly, Rosel closed the lesson book and told me to attend Sabbath services.

"You can read Hebrew there," she explained. "You'll follow along."

"At services? If I can't read the Shema — I surely won't be able to read the prayer book." My mind flashed to the pages and pages of tiny Hebrew text in temple. "There is no way I can read that."

"That's okay. You don't have to read. I think you'll be surprised by how much you know."

Rosel sat beside me the following Friday night, leaning over, dragging her finger along the prayer book passages for my eye to follow. I was thrilled to recognize a few words, and although I hadn't learned some of the alphabet yet, I was surprised by how much of the service I could follow.

"You're doing great!" Rosel whispered. "And these words are much smaller — without vowels!"

Rosel had explained to me that the Torah and many other Hebrew writings do not include vowels; the reader is expected to sight-read the word. I was proud of myself for being able to do just that. It occurred to me that I might actually be able to read Hebrew one day.

***

The weeks morphed from the cool days of spring into the heat of the summer. In addition to being the full-time mother of a preschooler and a baby, I was also meeting deadlines for my first writing job as events editor for three local magazines. Fitting Hebrew lessons into my schedule was challenging, yet it was an appointment I tried never to miss.

Often, small, thoughtful gifts waited for me on Rosel's table — a Jewish encyclopedia for Harrison, a Hanukkah picture book for Olivia, an article about the Jewish roots of Christmas, a container of homemade cookies. It was like entering the home of the grand-mother I'd always wanted. Even our family lines melded as Rosel asked about my parents and my siblings, my kids and my husband, and she introduced me to her life, too. Rosel told me that her eldest daughter wrote books and reviews about bed-and-breakfasts and that her younger daughter was a medical librarian and observed Conservative Judaism. She was proud of her grand-children, too — one granddaughter married a kind, handsome

Irish man while another married a modern Orthodox rabbi who taught at Columbia University. I looked for evidence of disappointment in Rosel's voice when she told me of the interfaith marriage of her granddaughter, or of her grandson who dropped out of college, but there was none. Rosel had led a life with unpredictable twists and turns, and it was as if she trusted that everyone else would find their way, too.

Raised in Bochum, Germany, Rosel moved to Rhode Island as a teenager during World War II. It was there that she met her husband, Arthur, and less than four months later, they were married. That was 64 years ago. As if that story wasn't romantic enough, Rosel told me that Arthur had built their house for her.

"I showed Arthur a picture of a house in the *New York Times* that I liked. He said, 'Find me a lot and I will build it for you.'" Although he had very little construction experience, he was intent on giving Rosel what she wanted.

"That was in 1959," Rosel continued. "The indoor pool was finished in 1962, in time for Sandy's sweet sixteen party."

"The kids must have loved that!" I said.

"We decided not to put any water in it, with all the kids around. But the boys loved running around the inside of the empty pool!"

Although he had been legally blind for years, Arthur often shuffled through the dining area during my Hebrew lessons, always stopping by the table to talk about current events. Taken with his intelligence and a broad smile that never waned, I loved the snippets of conversation with him. One day, while Rosel took a phone call, Arthur joined me at the table and told me he was very likely the luckiest man on earth.

"When I came here, I had nothing. But I always knew I would be all right."

"Did you have work when you arrived?"

"I was told there was no work to be had. That did not stop me." His eyes squinted behind thick, rectangular glasses.

"Then how did you find work?"

"I knew I would be hired if only they could meet me. So I went door to door to businesses until I found my first job."

Arthur told me that he invented collar stays and later became a self-taught architect, erecting several beautiful residences in Larchmont, including the rabbi's house. He was also one of the founders of Larchmont Temple, established at a time when Jews in Larchmont were meeting in a church space. Throughout his brief stories, Arthur continually described himself as lucky and fortunate. The rabbi had told me earlier that on every birthday, Arthur donates ambulances to hospitals in Israel. Yet Arthur's modesty would prohibit him from revealing that. He only wanted to live his life happily, something he succeeded at effortlessly.

As the months of study progressed, I found myself moved by Rosel's deep connection to her Jewish background. I knew little about my husband's heritage. Michael's father had avoided talking about his childhood, protecting himself from painful memories of a father who deserted the family, and of the hard work left to him in the wake of his departure. No one knew where the Friedeses came from... the best they could surmise was Eastern Europe. Bernice, whose own mother died when Bernice was 20, had a father who also expressed little about his past. The Jewish people had been through so much in order to survive, yet having no personal connection to the legacy myself, it all seemed a distant narrative.

That is, until Rosel told me her Holocaust story. She had just handed me an Internet printout, "Why I Am a Jew," and it opened a discussion that digressed from my Hebrew lesson, as happened so often in those hours.

"The war was breaking out around Europe. I was already here in the United States with my mother in 1937."

"Did you have family here?"

"My two sisters and my brother-in-law were already here. But not my uncle. Everyone told him to leave Germany. 'It's not safe,' they told him. But he insisted on staying."

"Could they have come later?"

"By then there wasn't time. But he could have sent his daughters to a kibbutz in Israel. Others were safe there. There was no reason not to send them."

"Why didn't he?"

"He wanted to keep his family together."

Rosel looked down at her hands, fingers knotted together. The situation was unimaginable. I couldn't envision making such a hopeless decision — keeping my children beside me with an invasion threatening, or sending them far away, not knowing if I would ever see them again. The very notion of it tightened my chest.

"Then September 1, 1939, the Nazis marched through my town. And my uncle and his family had to hide. But they also needed to eat. So they sent out my cousin, Susie."

"Wasn't that dangerous?"

"She had dark blonde hair and blue eyes. She looked Aryan, and they had sent her out before, so they believed it would be safe." Rosel paused. "She was 17. She never came back."

Rosel looked into my eyes placidly.

"Later, we heard that Susie was at a fruit stand. A Nazi called out, 'Hey, dirty Jew!' and she turned. It was just an impulse...." Rosel shook her head and looked down. "They shot her dead. Right there on the street."

I watched Rosel, looking for evidence of despair, something that mirrored the shallowness of my own breath — a tear, a shaking hand, a catch in her voice.

"She was my favorite cousin."

"Rosel... that's an unbelievable story." I tried to imagine the daily terror Rosel's family lived in while hiding from the Nazis, and the incredible courage it took Susie to risk her life to feed her family. That, along with the horror of the murder and the hatred it takes to commit such acts, were all incomprehensible.

My high-school history studies had included a week reviewing the Holocaust as part of the World War II curriculum. I had visited Dachau concentration camp while backpacking through Europe as a college student and had been unable to process the enormity of the mass murder even as I stood in front of the crematorium. Yet not until now, this moment, did genuine sorrow bring tears to my eyes.

I looked to Rosel, who was still shaking her head.

"I'll just never understand why my uncle didn't listen."

Through our conversations over the months, I was starting to weave together the common threads tying Rosel and Arthur, and Michael's friends and family. Although they were from disparate backgrounds, and they observed their religion to varying degrees, they shared their views on adversity and their sense of community. Rosel had mourned the death of family members who perished in the Holocaust, yet she expressed no bitterness and made it a point to contribute to charities on a regular basis. Arthur arrived in the United States an immigrant, told not to hope for success, yet he persevered with the brightest possible outlook. Michael's friend Beth lived with rheumatoid arthritis — a sometimes crippling disease — and recognized how fortunate she was to afford a nanny and top surgeons. Norman and Joan's house had nearly burned to the ground, yet they spoke gratefully about the few mementos they were able to rescue. The life of my mother-in-law spoke of endurance as well — a woman who had buried her husband and son and responded by devoting herself to volunteer efforts.

This outlook of perseverance and gratitude was what I had believed in all of my life. From being struck with bronchial pneumonia as a child to moving to New York City on my own as a college grad, I always acted on the assumption that I would be fine. Volunteering alongside my mother helping inner city families in Milwaukee, I learned to give back to the community. But these were very personal codes of behavior. Now, for the first time, I was surrounded by an entire culture that lived my beliefs.

At some point I knew I wasn't going to learn Hebrew with Rosel. My pronunciations were clumsy at best, and a workable vocabulary eluded me. But what I was starting to comprehend was far richer than mere language. I had come to Rosel to learn Hebrew, but instead, I had discovered something much larger. I was learning what it is to be Jewish.

Longing

"Dear, you know how I've been losing weight? And how my leg has been hurting?" Bernice had pulled me into our den as she was ending one of her Saturday visits to our home. Her expression tried to convince me she had something ordinary to tell me, but her hands clutching her handbag tightly told me otherwise.

"Yes..."

"The doctors are going to run some tests." She hesitated. "I'm sure its nothing."

"What do you mean, 'I'm sure it's nothing'? What are you saying?"

"Well, you know I had cancer about 20 years ago. I'm always a little nervous when things seem... abnormal."

I had dismissed the idea that my mother-in-law could be diagnosed with a terminal illness — she was the nucleus of our family. It was unimaginable that the strong, effervescent woman that stood before me could have any sort of sickness coursing through her body. But her test results revealed otherwise. Overnight our conversations went from grandchildren and weekend visits to oncology appointments, chemotherapy treatments, spinal taps, and CAT scans. As Bernice's medication took its toll on her body, we watched her rapidly transform from an athletic woman who played tennis twice a week to a frail person who needed several naps a day. Yet, as unmistakable as Bernice's declining health was, neither Michael nor Bernice's partner, Harold, could discuss the possibility of her dying. In the intimate circle of our family, it was a silent thought I carried alone.

Now, as I brushed my hair from my face hurrying through the doors of the temple, I was reminded of Bernice's illness. Eyeing the crowded sanctuary, I thought of *Erev Rosh Hashanah* and *Kol Nidre* — the evening High Holy Days services I attended alone with Bernice. I wanted her to sit with me in the temple again one day.

I focused on the task at hand — looking for a seat in the pews packed with people. It had been a feat to get out of the house at the kids' pre-bedtime hour. But tonight's program of cantorial singing at Larchmont Temple was an event I did not want to miss.

Even while Bernice's illness became part of my life, my mood lately was also buoyant, bubbling with Judaism. Just last month I had set my conversion date. As the rabbi predicted, one day I simply entered his study and announced, "I am ready to convert," as certain of that decision as I had been of my wedding vows.

Each book that I read solidified my sense of being Jewish. Several authors depicted Jews as passionate people struggling to understand their place in the world. I thought of my years of journal entries, trying to excavate my true talents in search of gratifying work, hoping to find a place where I could make my own unique contribution. Reading Daniel Gordis's description of Jews as people "on an honest searching," the word *honest* resonated with me. For the first time I respected my quest for purpose. Whether I found answers or not was irrelevant. Now I could honor my intentions.

In my year and a half of studying, my lessons had surpassed the fundamental values of Judaism. The basic principles had become rote to me. Now, rather than learning the broad concepts, I was deepening my inquiries. I analyzed the Torah portions with the rabbi and delved into interpretations. I continuously asked *why* things were written the way they were and listened intently to the theories. As my studies continued, a profound shift occurred. I was no longer studying to become a Jew. I was studying *as* a Jew.

When I told the rabbi I was ready to convert, he nodded, as if he had expected me to say this before I had entered the room. "I think that's wonderful," he smiled warmly.

"Where do we go from here?"

He jumped up from his chair and went to his desk, where he lifted a black, soft-covered day planner. "I have a thought..." I sat, giddy with anticipation, thrilled that we were actually discussing the date.

My decision was a gift beyond what I could have imagined. It wasn't long before this that I had questioned how anyone not born into Judaism could convert and authentically feel a part of the religion. Now I was planning my own date to officially become a Jew. My days of angst and conflict in my search for a religious home seemed a lifetime ago. It amazed me that such a shift had occurred, and I was grateful. With years of searching behind me, I had found my religion, my spiritual home for my family, and my community. I was settling into where I belonged.

"It's bashert!" the rabbi smiled. "Our Outreach Service is in two months, on February 11th."

Bashert, meaning *meant to be*, was one of my favorite concepts in Judaism. Often, as I reconstructed sequences of events, I saw how one incident or meeting fitted seamlessly into the other to create the perfect end result. If I hadn't answered the ad for a sales position at a magazine, I would never have met the receptionist, who became my friend, who later introduced me to Michael. Although the job didn't last long, it was still *meant to be*, as were my marriage and my new religion. I believed the more one surrendered to the idea of destiny, the more magic occurred. I loved that Judaism had a single word that synopsized a big part of my faith.

Still, I wasn't sure how the Outreach Service was related to my conversion. Did the rabbi expect me to convert in front of everyone? Was I to be a poster child for potential converts throughout the congregation?

"We could have your private conversion ceremony that morning."

I envisioned Michael, Bernice, and a few close friends gathering at the temple, sharing the intimate and deeply personal experience of my conversion. A private ceremony was exactly as it should be.

"Then, that evening, you and your family can come to services. To welcome you into the community as a Jew."

The schedule sounded perfect, except for the fact that I still felt like an imposter in the sanctuary. I was starting to feel Jewish in many aspects of my life. I was preparing Sabbath dinners most Friday nights, and I had joined the Social Action Committee at the temple to become involved in the community. Initiating a winter coat drive for immigrant families and expanding the holiday giving program, I was practicing mitzvot. Yet, ironically, the one place I decidedly did *not* feel Jewish was at services.

Now tonight, walking down the center aisle of the sanctuary moments before the cantorial celebration was to begin, I had pangs of homesickness for the church community of my childhood. Each Sunday, our family had entered Our Lady of Lourdes to be greeted by dozens of friends and acquaintances. Our favorite mass was held in the social hall, a casual room transformed into a place of worship every Sunday. I loved the informality, the low riser serving as an altar, the sections of gray folding chairs fanning out like the petals of a flower. The Struzynskis and the Wrobleskis were always sitting near the front, with the Sherwoods close by. My mother would already be at the pulpit, having arrived early to practice hymns with her ensemble for the guitar mass.

Even though I had attended Sabbath services a handful of times in the last year, as I settled into a pew to the right of the Torah, I still felt like an imposter in the sanctuary. Everywhere around me people greeted one another before taking their seats, exchanging kisses and handshakes. I was on the outside looking in. How could I convert if I still felt like an imposter in the temple?

I was hoping that tonight's service would be instrumental in changing these feelings. The cantorial singing had become one of my favorite components of services, my thoughts drifting to the spellbinding backdrop of operatic chanting, carried away by ancient melodies steeped in history. I was fascinated by the notion of Jews listening to this very music centuries ago, music still sung throughout the world today.

As the congregation turned to watch the clergy enter from the rear of the sanctuary, I saw that Susan, the rabbi's wife, was sitting in the pew in front of me. After the clergy reached the bema and we were all seated, I became fixated on the back of her head. I had spoken with the rabbi's wife in the corridors of the temple nursery school, but it was small talk. Susan was always in the center of a pod of girlfriends, enjoying the kind of banter that comes from years of shared experiences. Watching her at the nursery school, as well as observing her now, was a stinging reminder that I did not have these sorts of relationships at Larchmont Temple.

"It's really cold in here, isn't it?" I eavesdropped as Susan whispered to her girlfriend.

I looked down at my pashmina wrap, folded neatly next to my purse. I resisted the urge to tap her shoulder and offer it, knowing it would be my own desperate attempt to simulate a friendship.

Sitting in the sanctuary by myself, my sense of isolation grew. Congregants marveled and laughed at the cantor's anecdotes of her family and the songs they loved, and the rabbi made references that made no sense to me but elicited chuckles from everyone else. I felt as if I had wandered into someone else's family reunion. When Cantor Mendelson's husband joined her at the bema, rapturous as she sang into his eyes, a pang of envy overcame me. I was flooded with a desire for a marriage with shared spirituality. In the cantor and her husband, I saw an equal love for their religion, their joy in a sacred moment. It was moving to see a husband and his wife equally passionate about Judaism. I had been so grateful to find a religion of deep spiritual meaning to me. But now I realized that not only did I not feel at home in the temple, I didn't feel Judaism in my home, either. As I became more entrenched in my studies, I had imagined how wonderful it would be to have a husband enthusiastic about the Sabbath dinner, a husband who made it a point to come home before sundown on Friday night, grateful to leave the work week behind him, wanting only to revel in the intimacy of family and friends. I would have liked to experience a Saturday without shopping or running errands, choosing instead to spend a Sabbath playing with the children, relaxing with friends, shutting out all work and responsibility.

There was more I wished for: attending adult education together, volunteering in the community, talking about God — but I knew these were out of reach in my marriage. It's not that Michael had misrepresented himself. If anything, I was the one who had changed. Michael once joked, "I don't know what happened here. I thought I married a Catholic girl from Wisconsin and it turned out she's a Jew from Westchester!" He handled my change with grace, yet I couldn't help but wish he had accompanied me on my search.

The display of spiritual romance between the cantors, their visible adoration of their child, the faces of beaming congregants — these images started swimming around in my head, taunting me, telling me I was not ever really going to be Jewish. I might like what I was learning, but I would be isolated in my practice.

When services ended and everyone spilled into the anteroom for *Oneg Shabbat* and blessings, I broke free from the crowd and bolted for the side entrance. My sobs exploded with the push of the door as I navigated the cement staircase into the star-filled night. How ridiculous I was, thinking I could simply join this religion and feel I belonged! No matter how hard I tried, I would never have a historical frame of reference for the Jewish service. My family would never be a tight Jewish unit. If I had gleaned one thing from the evening of cantorial singing, it was that I was an intruder.

"How were services?" Michael called from the living room as I shut the door.

"Uh, all right." I grabbed a tissue, walking into the kitchen and dabbing my nose.

"Come here. Talk to me."

I entered the living room to find Michael reclining on the sofa, stockinged feet resting comfortably on the end cushion. He set his magazine on the coffee table.

"How was the sing—" he looked up. "What is it?"

"It's nothing. It's fine. Really." I shook my head, walking away again. "God, that table is so dusty. I really should clean it."

"How was the singing?" Michael called out. "Was it nice?"

I returned with a cleaning cloth and an aerosol can of furniture polish in hand.

"What are you doing?"

"I'm dusting."

"Since when do you dust at—"

I inhaled a sob, unsuccessful at concealing it.

Michael sat up. "What is it?"

My tears sprang free. "The thing is, I don't think I'll ever belong. I don't know why I bothered with all of this," I wept, as I moved picture frames around the oval table. "I'm not Jewish. I'll never be Jewish. I have *no idea* what is going on in that sanctuary." I moved to the deep windowsills, still spraying and pushing the cloth across the smooth, white wood.

"Well, honey," Michael laughed. "Neither do I. And I'm Jewish!"

I stopped dusting and looked at my husband. How I loved his humor and his candor. I plopped down next to him and slid into the crook of his arm.

"Really?" I cried.

"Really. It's all Greek to me. Or Hebrew, as it were."

I laughed.

"Why don't you talk to the rabbi?" he asked.

"I don't know if I should convert, Michael."

"Talk to the rabbi."

"I don't know if that will help."

He stroked my hair.

"Okay." I sniffled. "I'll talk with the rabbi."

***

The next morning, after scheduling my appointment, I ran into a close friend at the temple nursery school. Sylvia had converted years ago before getting married. While her conversion to Judaism was more cultural than spiritual, I felt lucky to have found her this morning when I was in a cloud of confusion.

"Sylvia," I called out to her, negotiating the ice patches on the sidewalk. "Do you have a minute?" I was surprised that I had tears to bite back.

Sylvia was continually busy, always with a professional project underway while managing her time volunteering in the schools and helping her husband with his business. Since we usually had to compare calendars a month ahead, I didn't expect to nab a slot of time this morning. But, before I knew it, I was sitting at her kitchen table, looking out onto the Long Island Sound while my friend poured me a cup of tea.

"Did you ever doubt your decision to convert?" I asked her.

"Absolutely. Especially right before I converted."

My relief was instant.

"Are you having doubts?"

"Well, not spiritually. I have no doubt that this is the religion for me. It's more cultural." I looked out onto the boats in the distance. "I don't think I'll ever belong."

"I know what you're saying. You're taking on a lot."

"Well, there's *that*, too. I mean, people ask me, *Why bother converting? Why not just raise the kids Jewish?*"

"I heard that," Sylvia said. "But for me, I wanted to keep the heritage alive. I *love* Jewish people. They're just so warm and genuine. And their history…we must never forget what Jewish people have endured. I wanted my kids to know that I feel very much a part of that."

I marveled at Sylvia's empathy. Striking, with strawberry-blonde hair, high cheekbones, and an athletic frame, her appearance reflected her strength and forthrightness. It was no wonder I had picked her out of a Newcomers' Club meeting and decided she had to be my friend.

"I haven't even thought about the anti-Semitism," I continued. "Have you experienced any?"

"Well, not directed at me. I almost feel like a spy for the Jews sometimes, since I hardly look Jewish. Once I was sitting in a client's office and he went off about Jews, making all kinds of ethnic slurs. He had no idea I was Jewish."

"Did you tell him?"

"Absolutely. I said, 'Well, you know *I'm* Jewish.' That shut him up."

"Well," I delved further. "What about feeling like part of the Jewish community? Do you now?"

"I definitely feel Jewish. But feeling part of the temple? No. But nor do I want to. It's just not important to me." Sylvia got up to pour more tea. "There all kinds of ways to be Jewish. You have to think about what's important to you."

I reflected on what Sylvia had said. It was not comforting: not only was I uncomfortable in temple; I would also be subject to anti-Semitism. Was this really what I wanted?

***

I didn't know how to tell Rabbi Sirkman that I was having second thoughts about my decision to convert. I loved everything I had learned about Judaism and was excited about all there was still to absorb. Yet thinking back to my experience in the sanctuary, my father's words haunted me. "They'll never accept you, you know."

I was riding in the passenger seat of my father's car. I had told him months earlier I was converting, and he had never voiced an opinion — until this very moment, during one of my visits to Milwaukee.

"Who won't accept me?"

"The Jewish people. I have two friends who are Jewish. They told me that you'll never really be accepted as a Jew."

"Well—" I looked directly at my father while he focused on the road— "that's just sad."

"Oh, yes," he nodded knowingly. "It is sad."

"I mean it's sad your friends feel that way. Pity the converted Jews who come their way, because I'm not experiencing that at all."

And I hadn't. There was no exclusionary behavior from any Jewish person I had met. No one snubbed me in conversation or dismissed my enthusiasm. On the contrary, from Michael's family to my rabbi to all of our friends, I had felt welcomed by each and every person who was Jewish.

I returned to the temple after talking with Sylvia, waiting in the hall for my appointment with the rabbi. I was profoundly confused. I was afraid that my faith wouldn't be enough to help me endure the isolation I still felt at temple or the prejudices awaiting me outside. As the minutes ticked by, I became more resolute that I was going to cancel my conversion. I could not see any way around it.

"Hello." I heard the rabbi's smile before he entered. I was always struck by how he greeted people, as if they were the greatest gift to him that day.

"Sit down, sit down."

We took our respective seats, he in his chair, me sinking into the loveseat.

"How are you?" As always, he asked like he meant it. Tears filled my eyes. Usually, it took me well into our session to have a tear or two trickle down my cheek, and then it was related to joy. Rabbi Sirkman could see this was different.

"What is it?"

"Rabbi," I bumbled through my words. "I don't know if I can convert." He handed me a tissue box. "I'm just so conflicted."

"Did something happen?"

"I went to the temple the night the cantors sang, and it was wonderful, and then it was awful, and the next thing I knew, I was home dusting."

"Dusting?"

"Well, crying and dusting. It's something I do when I'm upset."

The rabbi smiled, listening intently.

"Everywhere around me, people felt at home," I continued. "They knew each other. They knew the service." I gazed out his window at the trees, the very limbs I had looked out to during our first meeting when I described how God was everywhere for me.

"Rabbi, it was their home. I just didn't belong." I looked at my teacher. "And I don't. I don't know if I ever will."

His smile was like warm caramel. I didn't know how he could be taking my news so lightly. After all, he had personally escorted me down the path to Judaism, mentoring me, guiding me, watching me grow to love the religion he had dedicated his life to. I wondered if he didn't care that I might not convert, or if he simply did not hear the gravity in my voice. He leaned forward, clasping his fingers in front of him.

"I don't think it was a lack of belonging you were feeling." He looked steadfastly into my eyes. "It was a longing."

At that moment everything snapped into place like the click of a combination lock. The rabbi was right. It was a longing. I had felt it before — my yearning as a teenager to move to Manhattan, my calling since college to work on Seventh Avenue, the sensation that I belonged with Michael the instant I met him. I could see now that the feelings I experienced during services were the same. It wasn't that I feared feeling permanently out of place. I simply wanted to fast-forward to a time when I wouldn't. If my thirst for temple life was like my other longings, then I could trust that I was truly sitting in my home. I was experiencing my destiny *before* it was fulfilled.

Lightened by my realization, I settled into a discussion with the rabbi about the events of my conversion day, just a few weeks away. We would start and end the day at the temple, and he filled in the details in between. Thrilled once again at the prospect of my conversion, I got up from the sofa and pulled on my coat. I was filled with relief and comforted by my trust. I could put all of my uneasiness at bay. I was exactly where I belonged. My senses confirmed it.

"Before you go, I wanted you to do one more thing at your conversion," the rabbi said.

"Yes?"

"Speak at services that night."

"Speak at services?" I paused. Why couldn't I quietly become Jewish? People born into Judaism did not have to make any declaration about their faith, proclaiming themselves one of the tribe. Why did I? "But I just talked about my conversion last year. I wouldn't have anything different to say."

"You'll discuss your thesis."

I hesitated. That old nagging feeling that I had missed a piece of information crept up on me. "Thesis? What thesis?"

"Well, I've been wanting to talk to you about that. I thought it would be great for each conversion student to pick a Jewish topic and research it."

I was struggling through Hebrew, and I hardly felt graduate-level in my studies in Judaism. "I've never written a thesis before!"

"Oh, it's not a thesis, really. Just a paper — a discussion of your findings and your interpretations."

"How long does it have to be?"

"It doesn't matter — whatever it takes to complete it. Is there any topic that interests you?"

I thought about it a moment. The idea of probing deeper into one of the subjects in my readings had its appeal, and if I approached the topic more like a report than a thesis, it actually became enticing.

"Mitzvot. I'd love to explore mitzvot."

Performing mitzvot was very important to me. I attended the weekly Social Action Committee meetings at the temple and had done volunteer work on and off since I was a teenager. Yet I knew mitzvot included much more than good deeds. I wanted to explore the 613 laws that guided Jews in their day-to-day living.

"Wonderful. Now, let's look at the Torah portion for February 11th."

Since learning that the Torah was divided into 54 portions, I had become fascinated that Jews around the world study the exact same text on any given week.

The rabbi flipped a page of his calendar and slapped the open book with the back of his hand.

"It's bashert!"

"What is?" I tried to peek over the cover from a distance.

"The Torah portion is about *terumah*."

I shook my head, amazed. It was if I had picked curtain number two to find I had been granted the grand prize. Terumah, translated from Hebrew, meant a free-will offering from the heart, and it encapsulated why I was drawn to Jewish people. Everything about my conversion experience had been a free-will offering of other's hearts. Rabbi Sirkman's open door and generous spirit gave me a safe emotional place, and Rosel's selfless teaching of Hebrew while she shared her life both offered me countless lessons about Judaism. Michael's friends and family, enthusiastic about my joining their group, always asked me about my studies, authentically excited about my decision to convert. Friends at the nursery school, new faces at the Social Action Committee, all were openings of hearts.

Terumah was similar to the primary idea of mitzvot — charitable giving and helping others. I quickly wondered how the two concepts were different and why Judaism distinguished between the two. How was a free-will offering different from the Jewish law of helping others? I became excited about exploring the answers.

Indeed, it all seemed bashert. My conversion to Judaism transpired within two months of the annual Outreach Service. On the very day of my conversion, I would be performing a mitzvah, the good deed of sharing my experience with the community. It was *meant to be.*

"Free-will offering of the heart and mitzvah," I smiled. "What a wonderful way to start my Jewish life!"

Natural Waters

"How are you feeling?" Michael asked.

"Great. I feel great."

We waited in the temple hallway, perspiring in our winter coats.

"The rabbi will be just a few minutes," Cynthia told us, suggesting we wait outside the offices. "Are the kids with you?"

"Oh, no. They're with a sitter."

It was 9 am this frosty morning. By noon I would be Jewish.

I should have been tired. Anticipation had kept my mind racing the night before, and I had spent more hours awake than asleep. Finally, my yearning for a meaningful religion was being fulfilled. With the rabbi's words about longing, my doubts had been vanquished and my certainty about Judaism was unwavering.

I was excited about the possibilities for our family. In the last few weeks, Michael had made an effort to arrive home every Friday evening in time for Sabbath dinner, and I had tasted the cohesion that a Jewish life could bring. I thought it was romantic that we were learning the Sabbath blessings together and creating our own traditions, too.

Rather than use the customary blessing of the children, asking God to make our son like Ephraim and Menashe and our daughter like Sarah, Rebecca, Rachel and Leah, we placed a hand on our children's cheeks and praised them for specific things for the week.

"Olivia, we bless you and love you on this Sabbath. We think it's wonderful that you cleaned your toys in your room and played so beautifully with your brother...."

We danced to children's Shabbat music after reciting the *b'rachas*, scooping Harrison and Olivia into our arms. Their giggles worked their magic and erased the stress of the week.

My thesis studies on *mitzvot* made our Sabbath rituals even more meaningful. I learned that Shabbat is a time for the parents to reconnect with each other. Husbands are encouraged to whisper something lascivious in their wife's ear, and couples are required to make love on the Sabbath. Even if the couple hasn't spoken to each other in a week, the Sabbath is a time to find each other again.

Waiting for the rabbi in the hallway, I thought about the full day ahead of me — the *mikvah*, the *bet din* and my ceremony in the sanctuary would be followed by evening services, where I would read my d'var Torah in front of the congregation. The day would culminate in the Oneg, the gathering with pastries and wine after the service.

As momentous as the day was, my mother's presence made the day even more special. Her trip to New York for the sole purpose of witnessing my conversion moved me deeply. Though my mother had often seemed distracted in my childhood, her attention focused only on the sewing, cooking and cleaning, for my adult milestones, she was wholly present. She arrived hours early for my wedding, arranging tables and coordinating deliveries. For each of my children's births, she flew to New York to cook, clean, change diapers and take the 2 am feedings, all the while gently offering her maternal pearls of wisdom. Without question, whenever Michael and I moved house, she was there to unpack boxes, hang pictures, and help turn our house into a home.

Standing outside the offices of the temple, it struck me that the only person missing was Bernice. Weakened and fragile from her aggressive chemotherapy schedule, she had to preserve her energy for select outings. She had decided to meet us later for the private service in the sanctuary. "I want to be there the moment you become Jewish," she had beamed.

I saw a petite, blonde woman approaching me in the hallway. "Sally, how are you?"

"Dana!"

"Are you waiting to see the rabbi?"

"Yes." I paused for a moment, knowing I was about to take an awkward leap over small talk. "I'm converting today."

"You're converting today?" Standing easily eight inches shorter than me, Dana still managed to look intensely into my eyes.

I nodded, unable to contain my grin. "I am."

"That's *wonderful*. I so wish I could do it."

I was shocked to hear that Dana wasn't Jewish. As the chairperson of the Outreach Committee, she seemed an important leader in the temple. The few times I had attended Torah study, Dana was there, as she was at Friday-night services. I knew her husband was Jewish, and she was clearly a vital part of the synagogue.

"It's the most wonderful religion. Every time I have an *aliyah* and I stand on the bema facing the ark as the doors open, it's as if pixie dust sprinkles down from the Torah…it's so magical."

I thought about the Torah then, the scrolls standing on end in the majestic cabinet, and I wondered if one day I would be just as moved.

"Is there a reason you haven't converted?" I asked.

"I just couldn't. I love the religion, we're a Jewish family, my husband and I raise the kids Jewish. But I can't say for certain that Jesus isn't my savior." Her eyes teared. "I've been torn about it for years."

"Dana, it seems you've been able to be Jewish in your own way."

"I guess I have."

Dana's embrace caught me by surprise. "I don't know what your moments today will be, but this I know: it will be a special day."

***

"Welcome!" The rabbi greeted us, giving Michael and me hugs.

"Rabbi, I'd like you to meet my mother, Joyce. Mom, this is Rabbi Sirkman."

"It's wonderful to meet you." My mother extended her hand. The rabbi held it with both of his.

"It is great to meet *you*. Any mother of this incredible woman must be pretty incredible herself."

How odd it felt to see these two worlds joined — my mother, a leader in the Catholic church of my childhood, grasping the hand of the man who has ushered me into Judaism and into one of the most serious decisions of my adult life. Watching the gap effortlessly bridged reminded me that my life, although easily divided into segments, was indeed one complete picture. I wasn't leaving behind one life to transform into another. Rather, I was a composition — a Midwesterner, thankful for her religious home brimming with values, taking all that she loved about her upbringing into her adult spirituality, creating new roots in New York Judaism.

"Why don't we get started?" the rabbi motioned toward the door. "We can all ride in your car."

I took the front seat next to Michael, and we headed up Boston Post Road. Not surprisingly, my mother quickly jumped into a discussion with the rabbi, comparing Judaism and Christianity. I decided to tune the conversation out, taking in the leafless trees and the snow-splattered ground. The tones of winter formed a monochromatic palette, patches of gray ice blending into the concrete of the salt-caked streets. After a few wrong turns in

Connecticut, the rabbi directed us into the parking lot of a Conservative synagogue.

"It's back here," Rabbi Sirkman directed. "They're expecting us. The door should be open."

The four of us entered a room no larger than a walk-in closet. To the left, brass coat hooks jutted out from the wall. Straight ahead was a door that led to the mikvah.

"You can go right through there. The instructions will be on the wall. We'll wait here."

I hadn't known what to envision when I entered the actual room where I would submerge myself. I knew that mikvah meant "gathering of water," and that it usually held water that flowed from natural sources such as rainfall. In ancient times, men, women and priests used it to purify themselves before attending the holy temple. Today, the mikvah was most frequently used by Conservative or Orthodox women to purify themselves after their menstrual cycle. By doing so, they also connected to Jewish women who had been practicing the same tradition for the last 3000 years.

As I left my band of supporters and crossed the threshold to the pool, I had an eerie feeling of familiarity. I had never visited a mikvah before, and had certainly never set foot in this tiny corridor beneath this temple. I stood for a moment, trying to place the déjà vu. It was my wedding day. Standing alone in a room, my gown cascading around my feet, Michael had walked in.

"You look beautiful," he said, holding my hands. At that moment, eight years earlier, I was at the gateway between my single life and marriage. I stood then as I stood now, in a precise transitional moment.

The heated pool of pure rainwater was fed from a tank on the synagogue roof. To submerge myself, I had to remove all barriers between my body and the mikvah water, including all jewelry and makeup.

"I once brought a student here who was in there for 30

minutes. I couldn't imagine what was taking so long," the rabbi had recalled on the ride to Connecticut. "Only after she returned did I realize that she had followed every Orthodox rule for the mikvah, taking off her nail polish, cleaning her nails and more." He smiled. "You don't have to do that."

The atmosphere of the room was immediately calming. To my right glistened a pool no larger than 6 feet by 12 feet, surrounded by a beige tile floor. Soft lights dappled its surface, illuminating otherwise dark water. Above it, printed in large type on a white board, were two blessings written in Hebrew, their transliterations written below.

I undressed; hanging my clothing on the hooks mounted into the cinderblock wall, I stepped into the shower in preparation for immersing myself in the mikvah. I absent-mindedly checked my fingers for jewelry, forgetting I had already given my wedding and engagement rings to Michael for safekeeping. My mother held the solitary diamond necklace Bernice had given me when Harrison was born. I was stripped of all sentimental tokens, standing naked only as myself, no representation of past promises or future hopes. Simply me.

The mosaic tiles chilled the soles of my feet after the hot shower, and I welcomed the warmth of the water flooding over my skin as I stepped onto the first tread of the pool. Six more steps down the gracious stairs and I was in the center of the mikvah, now level with my chest. The only sound, the water lapping against the wall with each motion, made me acutely aware of my movements. For a moment I completely forgot that three people were waiting for me in the hallway, and I took in the quiet, the peace, the sound of the water tapping the tile.

I looked to the far wall and glanced at the blessings, and was glad that I had been allowed to keep my contact lenses in. Reviewing the words posted, I recalled the instructions given by the rabbi: *To be totally cleansed, one must immerse without touching any part of the mikvah.* Even in baptism, my three-week-old body had contact with people. My parents, the priest, my godparents all had their hands placed on me, guiding me through the ritual. I was also clothed in a baptismal gown. It is not often that one takes part in a ritual naked, returned to one's most natural state. Here, in the mikvah, I was as unadulterated as Adam and Eve before the fall.

Wanting to prolong the experience, I first floated on my back. Never being able to float comfortably for more than a few seconds, I was struck by how buoyant I felt in the natural water, as if invisible hands held me by the small of my back. I wanted to stay there, suspended and taking in the peaceful environment. Naked, stripped of all things artificial, I was not a wife nor a mother, not a daughter nor a sibling. I was simply myself, as I was born unto this earth. Time was static. I belonged to no one. Just as I had been carried to my birth in natural waters, so I was being carried to my spiritual rebirth. I was observing the tradition of visiting the mikvah, as women for generations had been doing, a time of renewal before venturing forth into the next month.

As much as I wanted to continue the magic of the mikvah, I had three people waiting for me in the corridor. I decided to begin my ritual.

I immersed my head, lifting my feet off the bottom, and resurfaced, then read the first two blessings aloud:

Praised are you, O Lord our God, King of the Universe, who has sanctified us with his commandments and commanded us with regard to immersion....

Praised are you, O Lord our God, King of the Universe, who has kept us in life, sustained us and enabled us to reach this time.

I immersed twice more, then reluctantly stepped from the mikvah and reached for the white, plush towels that awaited me. Pulling on my trousers and smoothing the fabric over my hips, I still did not feel ready to leave. I felt both rejuvenated and peaceful and wanted to sustain that moment a few minutes longer. The bright sunlight shocked me as I opened the door to the space where Michael, my mother and the rabbi waited.

"How was it?" Michael asked.

I touched my wet hair at the back of my neck. "It was...incredible."

Rabbi Sirkman nodded and asked me to stand beside him, placing my mother and Michael on either side of us.

"Sally, as you immersed in the living waters of new life, all of us pray that you will continue to drink from the waters of Torah, drawing henceforth from the wellspring of Jewish life, which will soon become your future."

As difficult as it was to leave the sanctum of the mikvah, the rabbi's words reminded me all of that lay ahead. Exploring the significance of the Torah and leading a Jewish life were ways of enriching my every day, and I was suddenly anxious to move forward. I pulled on my wool coat. I knew the bet din awaited me.

***

Literally translated, the Hebrew term bet din means "house of judgment." A convert must appear before a court of three Jewish people who believe in God, accept the theology of the Torah, and observe the mitzvot. These are the three requirements to convert. At least one member of the court must be a rabbi. The bet din has been interpreted as a safeguard; the court is there to question one's intentions in becoming Jewish, giving the convert a chance to bow out of the decision. The bet din may also deem the student's knowledge or intentions inadequate for conversion.

"Will there be a quiz?" I had asked the rabbi weeks earlier. "Do I need to know the books of the Torah? I don't exactly know the players. In fact, there is so much I don't know."

The rabbi had smiled. "It won't be a quiz. They will want to know what you have learned. Mostly, they'll want to know if this is the right move for you."

Knowing I performed better with preparation, I pressed on.

"Who exactly will be part of the bet din?"

"I'll take care of it. You'll see when you get there."

Working my damp hair into a ponytail, I left my mother and husband in the synagogue corridor and paused in the doorway of the rabbi's study. I was surprised that we were alone. Did the court forget it was my conversion day?

"Wait here. I'll be right back." The rabbi hastened out of the room. I sat in the chair and looked around at the vacant office, feeling uncomfortably alone. Whom had the rabbi gone to retrieve? Was he randomly assembling a panel? As always, I wanted the full, genuine experience — as I had in living off-campus in London so I could immerse myself in the city life, and as I had in giving birth to both of my children without medication. My bet din was no exception.

Although I had no trepidations about converting, I wanted to recap the magnitude of my decision. How did I feel about leaving my Catholic heritage behind? Did it bother me that I would have a different religion from my father, my brothers and sisters, my aunts and uncles, too? What did being Jewish mean to me? Did I really think I was qualified to lead a Jewish life, to raise my children in a Jewish household? I had asked myself all of these questions but never knew the answers. That was why I was looking forward to the bet din. I believed in its wisdom. I would be looking to the panel of Jewish leaders for confirmation and guidance.

The rabbi returned a few minutes later with his assistant rabbi and the cantor. Again, I was flooded with dismay. Why hadn't he brought in rabbis or leaders from outside of the synagogue? Didn't he want me to experience a serious questioning? Shouldn't someone who had no partiality to me be part of the bet din? After all, I was a member of the temple — were they really going to ask me pointed questions?

"Sally." Rabbi Rabinowitz extended his hand to me. He was the quintessential Jewish cleric, his salt-and-pepper beard and wire-rimmed glasses emblematic of his wisdom. Standing several inches shorter than me, everything about his demeanor was calming. I imagined what a gift he would be at a sick person's bedside. "An exciting day," he nodded.

I shook his hand, searching his eyes for evidence of having been caught off guard. Receiving only a steadfast look in return, I decided it was possible that I had been on his schedule.

"Hello, I'm Cantor Mendelson. It's good to meet you."

I remembered Fredda from the night of cantorial singing with her husband and son and from the few other services I had attended. Our association was one-way; I wasn't surprised she didn't recognize me. After the introductions, the three positioned themselves on the sofa, perpendicular to my chair, and waited for Rabbi Sirkman to begin.

"I'd like you to meet Sally Friedes. As you both know, Sally is converting today." He tapped his papers into a neat stack on the coffee table. "I could go on and on about Sally, but I'd like you to have the privilege of getting to know her yourself."

I smiled and looked to the rabbi and cantor. My court seemed, then, to be diminished to two. I resigned myself that the bet din wouldn't be the challenge I had hoped, and tried to hide my disappointment. I would have to take care of any remaining introspection on my own.

"Sally," Rabbi Rabinowitz began, "tell us why you are converting."

"The more I read," I told them, "the more I fell in love with the religion." The cantor and rabbi nodded. "But there was a time when embracing Judaism seemed an impossibility."

I was surprised to feel a knot in my throat as I thought about my road to Judaism. I told of meeting Michael, wondering what his exotic religion was all about, and becoming increasingly curious about Judaism. But, time and again, my curiosity had been met with roadblocks. Jewish people I questioned could offer me no insights to the principles of their religion and I was disillusioned when the rabbis at Central Synagogue and the 92nd Street Y renounced interfaith marriages.

Yet I was drawn to Jewish people. The women of National Council of Jewish Women embraced me, Michael's friends and family drew me in, and I loved being the daughter-in-law of a doting Jewish mother. It wasn't until I understood the significance of the High Holy Days that I caught a glimpse of the spirituality in Judaism. Once I started studying under the guidance of Rabbi Sirkman, I knew I had found my spiritual home.

"Sally," the cantor spoke, "were there any difficulties in making this decision?"

I reflected for a moment as the rabbi handed me the tissue box. One by one, my obstacles had vanished, including the ongoing angst about feeling like an imposter. If there had been any difficulty remaining, it was with Michael.

"Well, up until this morning, I suppose my husband has had a few issues with my conversion." Michael's messages had, indeed, been mixed. While his words declared his pride in me for converting, he had been reluctant to attend services with me.

"But he seems fine now. Today has made a difference," I added.

A few minutes before I entered the bet din, Michael confided in me that, at a stop on the way back from the mikvah, the rabbi had casually approached him about his concerns.

"For what it's worth," the rabbi had told Michael, "most spouses of converts feel a bit overwhelmed. Their enthusiasm can take you by surprise. It's completely natural," the rabbi had assured him. "But don't worry. Things will settle down."

It seemed that validation was all Michael needed to let go of his anxiety.

"And your family?" Rabbi Rabinowitz probed. "What do they

think about your conversion?"

I had let go of my past. My childhood religion did not fit who I was today. In this moment and over the last few months, I felt Jewish. I had forgotten that, to many people, my move from lapsed Catholic to Reform Jew was a radical change, and I suddenly appreciated my siblings' support and unwavering acceptance. When I had told my brothers and sisters, "We're going to be an interfaith family now," they said, "Great! We can learn so much!" I didn't have to give up my family, a vital part of who I was, to become who I wanted to be.

Throughout the questioning, a steady stream of tears trickled down my cheeks, each inquiry drawing up deep sentiments, reminding me of the incredible road I had taken to this very moment.

The tears stopped abruptly with the last question:

"What now?"

Rarely in any interview had I been stumped. My problem with job hunting had always been that I could give the perfect answers, thereby landing the job, without my discerning whether I actually wanted it or not.

The inquiry about my future as a Jew was different. It was a question I had posed myself, one to which, try as I might, I had no pat answer. What would I do now that I was Jewish? I was already active in the mitzvah of *tzedakah*, acts of charity, through my membership in the Social Action Committee, and I was slowly establishing a Jewish home by observing the Sabbath. I would also continue my Hebrew studies in hopes of actually learning the language. What else was there to being Jewish?

Looking into the eyes of three people who had devoted their lives to Judaism, who had spent countless years in rabbinical school studying Torah, Hebrew, philosophy and more, I saw in them something I envied and desired: knowledge.

"Study. I want to continue my studies in Judaism, starting with regular attendance at Torah study."

"Of course, rabbinical school is always an option," Rabbi Sirkman had chimed in.

I was shocked. He had spoken what had grown from a wistful thought to a secret desire. Did he actually think I could become a rabbi?

"I can't envision a better job." I looked to my bet din duo, my eyes filling up again. "Imagine spending your days doing so much for others because it's what you love to do. Then getting these incredible gifts — insights, love, wisdom — from others." Rabbi Rabinowitz looked surprised, as if hearing this viewpoint for the first time. "You think your helping others is reward enough, then God gives you tenfold in return. Life is magical that way. As rabbis, you get to witness the miracle of the human spirit every day. I can't picture a more fulfilling way to spend one's life."

Rabbi Sirkman smiled, looking at the others. "See what I mean?"

As we all stood and hugged, their words lifted me up: "*Mazel tov*." The interview from the bet din gave me the gift of certainty. I saw that my conversion did not pull me away from my brothers and sisters — it added another dimension to our family. Their acceptance of my decision made me love them all the more. I also realized then that the bet din was not designed to answer the panel's questions. Its purpose was to satisfy mine.

Leaving the rabbi's study, greeting my family with crumbling tissue in hand, this was the last time I would exit my mentor's study as a non-Jew.

The New Jew

Hundreds of faces looked at me expectantly as I stood at the bema, hands resting on the podium. My breathing slow, my gaze relaxed, I was conspicuously comfortable there, and I was in no hurry to speak. The events of the morning, while seeming so long ago, still echoed within me.

I had exited the rabbi's study after the bet din to be welcomed by one of the most adoring voices in my life.

"Hello, dear!"

Bernice approached me, her mink coat hanging from her tiny frame. She leaned into her cane, and her elegant fingers reached for my cheek. The cancer may have sapped her strength, but her scent and touch were unaltered.

"Were you waiting long?" I leaned forward, accepting the warmth of her kiss.

"Oh, no! We had plenty of time to stop by the house to see Olivia before we picked up Harrison."

"Mommy's here!" Michael called down the hall.

Harrison broke away from my mother's side and tore down the corridor into my arms.

"Mommy! Where were you?"

"I was talking with the rabbis, sweetie."

As the rabbi directed us up the stairs to the sanctuary for my private service, Michael looked startled when Bernice eased herself into the chairlift mounted to the railing.

"Mom, do you really need that?"

"Yay! I want to ride with Nana B.!" Harrison reached for his grandmother.

I touched Michael's arm. "It's okay, honey."

I was struck by how eerily quiet and hollow the sanctuary seemed, so different from the usual bustling atmosphere of Friday night services or the High Holy Days. I was reminded of weekday visits with my mother to Our Lady of Lourdes, when I felt both privileged and a trespasser as we walked through the uninhabited church. I often found myself breathing quietly so I would not be noticed. Now my mother was here with me in my hushed sanctuary.

But we weren't alone at Larchmont Temple. Sitting in the first few rows were three diminutive forms — Rosel and Bernice's friends Jerrie and Dan. Cantor Mendelson had managed to get to the sanctuary before us, and she stood on the bema, the hem of her white robe brushing the carpeted platform.

"Join me on the bema, Sally." The rabbi waved me toward the front.

As the cantor sang in Hebrew, the rabbi escorted me to the ark and opened its doors. I had never stood this close to the Torah before. It was as if the rabbi were personally introducing the Torah and me. I did not experience the pixie dust Dana described, but I felt a deep sense of the gravity of this meeting, which was only enhanced by the cantor's operatic singing. I was establishing a significant relationship with the Torah. For thousands of years it had been the text of the Jewish people, the guidepost for their lives. Although they tired of building temples that would only be destroyed, they never gave up the Torah, keeping the sacred texts wrapped and safe as they journeyed through the desert. The Torah was no less important today, and as I gazed at it under the lights of the ark, I looked forward to discovering its magic.

Closing the doors of the ark, the rabbi brought me back to the center of the bema. "The Shema is our declaration that we have faith in one God," he explained. "Because it is a central prayer in

Judaism, it is customary to recite it at one's conversion."

I reached in my pocket and pulled out a folded piece of paper. Typed on it were phonetic spellings of Hebrew words. While I had practiced hard to memorize the prayer, or at least be able to read the Hebrew words fluently, I had fallen short of both goals. Yet the Shema resonated with me deeply. From the first time I read the blessing with Rosel, I was struck by its simplicity and clarity. My own belief in everything it commanded was amplified with each word.

"*V'a-hav-ta et Adonai eh-lo-heh-cha b'chol l'va-v'cha...*" The Hebrew transliteration flowed more fluidly from my lips than I had expected. "And you shall love Adonai, your God, with all your heart and with all your soul..."

For the first time, I understood what was meant by "The Lord is my shepherd," the twenty-third Psalm I had recited as a child. Standing on the bema, the rabbi at my side, I had a solid trust in God. Finding Judaism was not happenstance: I had been led to it. My entire journey brought me to this moment. If I hadn't moved to New York, I would not have met Michael, his family and his friends. It was their Jewish culture that piqued my interest. Because I was raised by a mother who continually explored her own spiritual path and included me in the process, I had the courage to do my own searching. If Jerrie and Dan hadn't recommended the realtor who brought us to Larchmont, I wouldn't have stumbled upon the temple and met the rabbi who could finally make Judaism meaningful to me personally. With my sense that this was all bashert, I could trust that I would always be led where I needed to go.

"*V'ha-yu ha-d'va-rim ha-ei-leh a-sher a-no-chi m'tza-v cha ha-yom al l'va-veh-cha...*" Swept away by the power of the blessing, I was trying before I even spoke the second verse. "And these words which I command you today shall be in your heart." The Shema was imploring me to feel in my heart the words of the commandments set forth in the blessing. And felt them I did, because the words rang so true.

"And you shall teach them diligently to your children. And you shall speak of them when you sit in your house and when you travel on the road..." I looked at my mother smiling warmly at me and was overcome with gratitude. My journey was so different from hers, yet here she sat in a foreign environment, present in the synagogue because she was genuinely happy for me. I was grateful I could share my faith with her. Speaking of my beliefs with others was precisely what the Shema was commanding me to do. While I had no hesitations in teaching Judaism to my children, I hadn't yet taken the chance to express my spirituality to my friends and family. Study, meditation and introspection were all very good, but it is in sharing ourselves that our spirituality comes alive. If I wanted to breathe in the beauty of spirituality, I was going to have to breathe it out as well.

"And you shall bind them for a sign upon your hand..." I thought about the generous gift of my tallit from a congregation member, who brought each convert to a nearby Judaica shop to select a prayer shawl. "You'll know which tallit belongs to you when you try it on," she told me, and she was right. The minute I draped a soft, white shawl with stripes of metallic gold and gradient grays around my shoulders, it was as if I were wrapping myself in Judaism. I twisted the knotted fringe from its corners around my fingers, and grasped my faith tightly.

"And you shall write them upon your doorposts of your house and upon your gateways." The frame of Bernice's front door held a *mezuzah*, as did Norman and Joan's and many of Michael's friends' entryways. When I learned from Rosel that the parchment inside the small case was inscribed with the Hebrew Shema, our mezuzah became even more meaningful. Each time I passed it as I entered my home, I was reminded of my faith, and I remembered who I was as I left — a loving, open woman who tried to live her life by Jewish principles.

"Does anyone have a tissue?" I asked the mothers in the pew

after I finished my reading. Four sets of hands opened purses.

"I need one, too," Bernice smiled.

The mitzvah of sharing this occasion came to life in that moment. My journey may have been a personal one, but in the soft expressions of the others, I saw that they, too, were profoundly touched by my becoming Jewish.

The rabbi waited a moment, then turned to me. "Sally," the rabbi said. "You have cleansed in the mikvah, sat before the bet din, accepted blessings and recited the Shema. You are ready to continue your life as a Jew."

It had been an incredible road to conversion. Leaving my Catholic roots, I had searched for years for a spiritual home. My yearning had brought me to various churches, none of which offered me what I needed. Hoping my husband's faith might fit, I explored Judaism, only to be left repeatedly discouraged — until I came upon Larchmont Temple. Now, after nearly two years of study, I was going to leave my role as student and become part of the Jewish community.

"Before you share in the embraces of your friends and family, I want to give you something." Rabbi Sirkman pulled a book from a shelf beneath the podium. I immediately recognized the author as one of the most renowned contemporary Jewish scholars. "I have never given this book to anyone before. It was written by my mentor, and I give it to you today, knowing you are ready to study Torah." Overcome with emotion, I whispered a barely audible "thank you," and hugged my teacher.

As the cantor led everyone in singing and clapping to *Siman Tov u Mazel Tov*, Harrison ran up to the bema and climbed into my arms. My journey to Judaism had ended. My search, my studies, the trepidations were all behind me. I had entered the sanctuary as a woman in transition. I stepped off the bema as a Jew.

***

Now, just hours later, I stood at the podium, studying the faces in the pews of the crowded sanctuary. Friends from Larchmont and Manhattan, congregants, Michael's family and my mother had all come to the synagogue this wintry evening to celebrate my conversion. A brief pang of sadness tugged at me as I felt Bernice's absence. Her energy had waned during our earlier luncheon, and she'd decided to return to the comfort of her apartment to rest. I would have loved to see her maternal pride as I gave my *d'var Torah* from the bema, yet I was grateful she had been there for the most important part of the day — the moment I became Jewish.

"This week's Torah portion is about terumah — the free will offering of the heart," I began. "The Lord asks that an offering be made from every person whose heart so moves him. This is apart from our Jewish law of tzedakah, our obligation to contribute."

In trying to find a natural connection between the Torah portion of terumah and my thesis topic of mitzvot, I questioned the requirement of making an offering only if we are genuinely moved to do so. How often did moments of inspired giving occur? Did we have to wait for these moments of inspiration for our hearts to be opened? I referred to my readings and realized we had been given a way to increase the number of "aha" moments in our lives. In fact, one might actually consider it a list of methods to increase inspired moments when our hearts would open. The key was mitzvot, and we had 613 of them.

"When I began my study of Judaism I believed mitzvah meant 'good deed,'" I continued. "But I've come to learn that it is so much more than that. It is tradition, spirituality and faith all rolled into one."

I described my first felt experience of mitzvot on Yom Kippur when I was pregnant with Olivia. Michael, Bernice and I sat down to dinner after lighting the *yahrtzeit* candles in the dining room, one in memory of Michael's brother and the other in memory of his father. I thought it was a nice tradition, a lovely moment to remember two people who have passed away. I was the first one up the next morning, and as I passed the entry to the dining room, I stopped short, and I cried. I saw the two candles still flickering on the sideboard and felt the spirits of Tony and Harry burning brightly in our home. They had been with us all night as we slept and were there to greet us in the morning. With Bernice sleeping in the guest bedroom, and Michael and the children down the hall, I felt like our whole family was together in the house.

"I didn't know it at the time, but by performing a mitzvah, I experienced it."

I confessed that in studying mitzvot, I started to ask myself why I wasn't more observant of the Jewish commandments. If they were opportunities to let God in, why not open the door? I knew many of the people I was speaking to shared my hesitancy — if it didn't seem logical, we didn't do it. Keeping kosher, saying blessings throughout the day, ceasing any type of work on the Sabbath — the inconveniences seemed to outnumber the payoffs.

"The irony is," I explained, "many Jews who consider themselves nonobservant or even adverse to Jewish rituals are already unknowingly performing mitzvot. You simply know no other way."

Almost every Jewish person I knew was involved in charitable causes, writing checks to nonprofit organizations and volunteering their time. Although they may not have defined it as such, they were observing the mitzvah of tzedakah. Celebrating milestones with the community was also standard in the Jewish community. From baby namings and brises to b'nei mitzvahs, birthdays, anniversarys and deaths, Jewish people rarely, if ever, celebrated significant events alone. It was a mitzvah to share life-cycle events with the community.

In preparing my talk, I had thought back to when I'd criticized Jewish people for having no concept of what their religion was about. No matter how much I questioned friends and family, they could not tell me about the principles of Reform Judaism. I saw now that they really had understood their religion and their culture. They were just so embedded in living Judaism, they couldn't verbalize it.

"You just performed a mitzvah tonight, accepting a convert, welcoming me into the congregation and the Jewish community as an equal." I looked up from my notes, into the faces of my fellow Jews. "By your being here with an open heart, I will be able to see myself as a Jew and raise my children in a Jewish home. It is a gift to me and my children and the generations to come."

As I stepped off the bema, passing the pews filled with friends, family, and congregation members, I was stepping into my Jewish life. Torah studies awaited, as did social-action projects, Sabbath dinners and more.

Slipping into my seat, Michael touched my knee. "You did great, honey."

I grinned. "Thanks."

"Guess what?" he asked.

"What?"

"You're Jewish."

Sitting next to my husband in the middle of the sanctuary, my mother on my other side, surrounded by my New York friends and family, I knew it wasn't as simple as that. I was many things. I was a Catholic girl from Wisconsin who cherished her upbringing in a big family. I was an adventurer and a dreamer, who had moved to New York to find her glamor girl within. I was a devoted mother, a loyal friend, a loving wife, and an aspiring writer. I was an advocate for the poor and an optimist for the future. I was all of these. And now I was something else as well. I was a Jew.

Epilogue

I cursed myself for leaving the house so late yet again. I had to get Harrison and Olivia settled in childcare, and I finally arrived upstairs in the sanctuary just minutes before Rosh Hashanah services were to begin. I stood in the back, eyes searching for Michael in the mass of people.

"Sally! L'shana tova!"

"Shana tova!" I hugged friends from the preschool.

"I think I saw Michael up front," they said, motioning. Before I could spot him, another arm reached for me.

"Shana tova!" Rosel greeted me. "Arthur, it's Sally."

"Happy New Year, Sally!" Arthur chimed in.

"Happy New Year, Rosel and Arthur. I'm so happy to see you."

"L'shana tova!" the chairperson from the Social Action Committee kissed my cheek.

"Shana tova, Lee!"

Pulling away from his hug, I caught sight of Michael waving at me from across the room, handsome in his navy suit, and tried to make my way to him. Organ music started and I knew my time was limited, but getting through the crowd became difficult. Everywhere I turned, I saw people to embrace. Members of the Social Action Committee, friends from Torah study, parents from the preschool, neighbors, and even our real estate agent and her husband.

"Boy, that was like the parting of the Red Sea," Michael said when I finally reached him. "Here. Don't forget this."

I unfolded my tallit from its velvet case, blessed it, and wrapped it around my shoulders. I gazed at my husband, loving how he looked in his yarmulke. It wasn't that long ago that he seemed exotic and foreign wearing it.

As the service began and I settled into the pew, I opened my prayer book to the morning service.

"Praised the Eternal One, O my soul! O God, You are very great!"

The rabbi stood at the pulpit, the cantor at his side. I thought how wonderful it was to sit here in the pew, looking at the bema that felt familiar to me. Glancing down at my book, I found the passages where the rabbi was reading. When he spoke Hebrew, I followed along, able to catch every third word while keeping pace.

I flipped back to the meditations, the same pages that had drawn me in years ago at Central Synagogue. I wrapped the tallit fringe around my fingers and immersed myself in their thought-provoking verses to the backdrop of the cantor's singing. Before I could get to the third meditation, I heard the call of my favorite blessing.

Shema, Y'Israel, Adonai Eloheinu, Adonai Echad!

Michael pointed to his page number and my eyes scanned my book for the beginning of the Shema.

V'a-hav-ta et Adonai eh-lo-heh-cha b'chol...

Without warning, I felt a burning heat behind my eyes, a sign that tears were about to follow. The last time Michael and I were together when I recited the Shema was on my conversion day. It was the last time Bernice had been in the sanctuary with us. The sound of the Shema recited by the congregation faded, and all I could see was Bernice's radiant smile from the pew as I stood on the bema. We didn't know then that within a month of that day, she would be gone.

♦ I had known Bernice was dying, but because Michael hadn't been able to talk about the inevitable, her illness too reminiscent of the deaths of her brother and father, I found myself crying alone late at night, looking out of the den window into the winter darkness or holding sleeping Olivia in my arms after an early morning bottle.

I needed a way to keep Bernice with me after she left us.

I wouldn't be able to honor my mother-in-law by naming a child after her; Michael and I were finished having children. But I could honor her with my own name. When the rabbi told me I needed to pick a Hebrew name, I knew immediately that it had to be Ruth. A biblical figure who was a devoted daughter-in-law, Ruth traveled with her late husband's mother across the desert, working hard in the fields to support her. I would have done no less for Bernice. In taking Ruth as my Hebrew name, I had gone one step further than honoring my mother-in-law — I was honoring our relationship.

When I ran into the rabbi outside the temple one snowy morning before my conversion and told him of my choice, he smiled and said, "I thought you would pick that name."

"Really?" I was astonished. "Because Ruth was a devoted daughter-in-law?"

"Not only that," he smiled. "Because she was also the first convert."

It had been bashert.

ACKNOWLEDGMENTS

If there is one thing I love to write, it is a thank-you note. This letter is to all those in my life who enriched the telling of my story.

To my dear friend, mentor, teacher and confidante, Jane Anne Staw, I owe a debt of gratitude. Thank you for your gentle guidance, warmth and compassion. Most of all, thank you for being a constant through all the changes in my life and for seeing me through those transitions. This book would not have been written without you.

Thank you, Michael, for always believing in me. It was you who enrolled me in my first writing class and convinced me that my story was worth telling. Olivia and Harrison, my incredible children, your names in the front of this book are not enough to tell you how grateful I am for your unbridled enthusiasm. From my first draft to publication, you were always there cheering me on. To my mother, my role model in so many ways, thank you for your unfaltering support. Your positive feedback made it easy for me to believe in myself. It is quite powerful to know that my mother is my number one fan.

To my friends and family — Steve, Chris, Dad, Liz, Raegan, Stephanie, Chrissy, Lisa, Dana, Jeff, Nina, Robin, Sylvia, Karen, everyone at McCutcheon, and the countless others too numerous to name — I thank you for your endless support. Writing can be an isolated and private experience; each time you checked in with me I was reminded that I was not alone.

To the wonderful staff at O-Books; to Susan Weiss, my tireless and gifted copy editor; to Larry Kushner, my advisor; to James Hall, my talented photographer; and to John Sternig, the visionary who designed the book cover — thank you for guiding me through the last leg of my journey.

Thank you, Bernice, for the impact you had on me. Many times while writing this story, I felt you near my desk or saw you smiling lovingly from across the room. Thank you for staying with me even after you've gone.

Finally, thank you, God, for escorting me on this and every journey, and for nudging me to write this book. Each page I wrote was an adventure that revealed new insights, memories, and hopes. The process gave me faith that I can face all the unknown adventures that lie ahead.

BOOKS

O is a symbol of the world, of oneness and unity. In different cultures it also means the "eye," symbolizing knowledge and insight. We aim to publish books that are accessible, constructive and that challenge accepted opinion, both that of academia and the "moral majority."

Our books are available in all good English language bookstores worldwide. If you don't see the book on the shelves ask the bookstore to order it for you, quoting the ISBN number and title. Alternatively you can order online (all major online retail sites carry our titles) or contact the distributor in the relevant country, listed on the copyright page.

See our website **www.o-books.net** for a full list of over 500 titles, growing by 100 a year.

And tune in to myspiritradio.com for our book review radio show, hosted by June-Elleni Laine, where you can listen to the authors discussing their books.

MySpiritRadio